Squigglesprout

Bibliographic Information:
Author: Greg Schlueter (b. 1967)
Title: Primal Fire
Description: First U.S. edition.
Publisher: Squigglesprout, Holland, Ohio, 2025
Identifiers:
ISBN: 979-8-9923353-2-3 (Paperback)
ISBN: 979-8-9923353-5-4 (eBook)
Cover Art and Design:
Created by Greg Schlueter
© 2025 by Squigglesprout, Holland, Ohio.

Bulk Orders:
Our books may be purchased in bulk. Please contact us at
Piglets@Squigglesprout.com for more information.

Dedication

For every restless heart
that has stood on a stage,
or in a silence,
and whispered:
There must be more.
From the dark wood to the open sky,
from Inferno to Paradiso—
this story is for all of us
making the climb.

As I gazed on her, my soul was stirred
By love that moved the sun and other stars.
But my own wings were not enough for this,
Had it not been that then my mind there smote
A flash of lightning, wherein came its wish.
Here power failed the lofty fantasy;
But now my will and my desire were turned,
Like wheels revolving with an even motion,
By love that moves the sun and other stars.

—Dante Alighieri, *Divine Comedy: Paradiso*,
Canto XXXIII, 139–145 (trans. Allen Mandelbaum)

Chapter 1: Dance of Desire

The Columbus warehouse pulsed, its brick and steel trembling under four thousand souls pressed tight, their heat a haze of spilled beer and raw longing. At its center stood Dante Johnson, sweat-soaked, his voice ragged as a broken vow, sinking low like a dying sun only to soar like a hawk. It tore through *Dance of Desire*, the anthem that had scorched its way from Ohio dives to Pacific highways, a cry that bound the crowd into one writhing beast. Their chant rose, a primal hymn: *Take the floor—Dance of Desire! Wanting more—Feel the fire!*

Two years ago, he'd scrawled it in a bourbon blur, chasing a girl whose eyes dissolved by dawn, her name lost to the bottle. Now it was a flame he wielded, fierce but untamed. A girl with purple-streaked hair swayed, eyes glistening, arms grasping the air as if underwater and salvation hung just out of reach. Beside her, a boy with scars etching his jaw moved with her, their fingers grazing. They weren't here for a concert—they were here to be consumed, to let the music's anesthetic current rush over wounds they hid even from themselves.

Dante poured out everything—voice, sweat, soul—his boots grinding the stage's weathered oak, the mic a searing brand against his lips. He saw them, not as faces but as fractures: a boy screaming to drown a father's rage, a woman writhing to erase a lover's betrayal, a generation chasing ghosts of a Woodstock dream long buried. The warehouse was their cathedral, the music their absolution, each breath a promise of release. Yet beneath the blaze, a shadow stirred: *What am I chasing?* It flickered, then drowned in the crowd's roar, but its echo lingered, a tide pulling toward a shore he couldn't name. But he wasn't ready to leave.

Fred's bass resonated deep, a thrum carved in earth, steady as stone. Doc's drums roared, a stampede tearing across scorched plains. Jax's guitar slashed, bright and jagged, while Nico's keys were something almost amniotic, a warm sea you could drown in. Their sound was a brotherhood, a fire that burned brighter together, but along with it, increasingly, Dante felt the pull of something like a shadow, its whisper disconcerting but seductive, echo growing in his depths.

The set crashed down, the reverberation clinging like smoke. Backstage was a labyrinth of coiled cables, stacked plastic cups, bottles and snack wrappers. Dante handed his mic to a stagehand, ears ringing. Women swirled around him, moths to a flame, their eyes bright with hunger, their laughter brittle as shattered glass. He knew that fire, had tasted its heat, but tonight, along with the shadow, something else stirred, faint, like a river's hymn, whispering something else.

The greenroom buzzed with heat and noise. Fred tipped back a dented Metallica water bottle, cropped hair slick with sweat, his grin sparking like a live wire. Jax flung his leather jacket over a chair, his eyes flicking to a promoter lingering beyond, as if he could already see his name in bigger lights. Nico slumped against the wall, pale as ash, fingers tracing his synth case, sketching a figure in a battered notebook—half-erased, eyes like voids. Doc strolled in, red beanie skewed, towel draped over his shoulders, his sly grin warm but piercing, the rosary tattoo on his forearm glinting. "You holdin' up, jefe?" he asked, his Mexican accent curling like incense, eyes catching the shadow Dante tried to hide.

"Yeah," Dante said, catching the water bottle Doc tossed, forcing a smile that didn't reach his eyes. "Still ridin' the storm out..." The REO Speedwagon quip landed soft, their shorthand for the afterglow, when the crowd's thunder still resounded.

2

Doc's gaze lingered, seeing through the mask, but he let it slide, turning to jab sarcastically at Jax's "all-thumbs" solos and Fred's "freight-train" bass, the banter biting as a brotherly backslap.

Jax smirked, restringing his Gibson without looking up. "Better thumbs than all talk, El Cartel."

Doc grinned like he'd been handed a prize. "Finally, some respect."

Fred snorted, plucking a low run, his face stone but warm. "Subtle gets it done. Like your last drum fill, Ramirez."

Doc raised his hands, "Careful, lumberjack. I got cousins who bury bassists in the desert."

Fred didn't flinch, "They'd have to catch a little of this first," leading into an impressive slap bass run.

Jax leaned back, grinning. "Bro, your fingers fly, but the rest of you's about as lively as Entwistle... in the ground."

Laughter broke loose, quick and unguarded, a current Dante couldn't ride. Vince stormed in, suit rumpled, voice booming. "Verge Records is circling, boys! National tours, fat stacks, the works!" His words painted visions of arenas, his tie loose like they were already there.

Fred glanced at Doc, deadpan. "Think how many tacos you could buy."

Doc chuckled, low and warm. "Long as ICE don't raid the greenroom."

Laughing, Vince pinched the bridge of his nose, exasperated.

"You'll thank me when you're legends."

"Legends?" Fred shot a look at Jax, shoulders rolling into a bluesy walking bass line to punctuate his point.

3

"For this guy? Maybe in debauchery."

Even Nico cracked a faint grin, his pencil pausing over the sketch.

Dante barely registered it, the crowd's chant—*Wanting more*—swallowing Vince's words, the shadow sharpening into a question he couldn't shake. He slipped out to the alley, the night air biting his sweat-slick skin, Columbus sprawling beyond—brick walls scrawled with time's graffiti, streetlamps bleeding yellow, the Scioto River's faint shimmer winking under a sagging moon. The city's pulse felt remote, a low thrum rising, and beneath it, softer still, a whisper of light: *There must be more.*

His apartment waited, a refuge from the world's churn—open mics, a viral clip, Primal Fire's rocket rise—a life of parties and paper-thin adulation that increasingly felt less like glory and more like a script. Inside, the walls were a shrine to the rockstar dream: Steve Perry mid-*Faithfully*, Eddie Vedder's snarl, Van Halen's fingers blurring, Marcus Mumford's fervent croon. Vinyl stacks teetered; a chipped Gibson mug sat by cigarette burns on the couch.

Dante's boots rasped a refrain across the worn floor, passing the unmade bed where a woman had slipped away that morning, her scent of jasmine and regret lingering. Her note on the pillow—"I'll never forget you"—stared back, a mirror to his own emptiness, a well-rehearsed role he'd been playing never asking who wrote it or where it led. In the quiet, a melody continued to stir, faint as breath, whispering of a truth beyond the stage. Rising from those depths he could hear Seger's weary voice crooning to him, about playing star again. Yearning to break free.

He sank onto the frayed carpet by the window, beside the guitar he called "Runkle," a name born from his ten-year-old self's misstep, blending "Rich" and "Uncle" David, who'd pressed it into his hands with a prophecy: "You're not made for toys, Dante. Music's in your soul. You're meant to set the world on fire. Here's the spark." The guitar was a relic of that promise, its strings a lifeline to songs born in silence.

In the dark, Dante's fingers traced the wood's grain, the night's stillness a canvas for a melody stirring within—a fragile thread of truth the stage threatened to unravel, a question he couldn't yet answer: *Is there more?*

Chapter 2: Echoes in the Ruins

Morning stole into the apartment like a thief, light seeping through crooked blinds, pooling on the couch where Dante had crashed. The air hung heavy with stale coffee, grounds scattered across the counter. Doc's snores rumbled from the hall, a steady rhythm amid the clutter—eggshells cracked open, a half-eaten taco abandoned, a guitar pick wedged in the floorboards.

Dante snatched his hoodie from a chair, his gaze catching the shelf by the window, where frames held living ghosts: Grandpa Michael's wise face beside Grandma Catherine's warmth, her eyes a beacon of faith he'd never seen but felt in family tales, a glimmer of Lake Diane's dawns; his parents, Paul and Maria, laughing at a church picnic, their joy warm as the morning sun; his older siblings, Ben's bold grin, Tessa's gentle delight at lakehouse gatherings, guitars and violins echoing cousins' songs; Aunt Anna's devout and loving countenance, her listening heart a sanctuary of care since marrying Robert, their daughter Sophia—more than twelve years his elder—checking in like a big sister, her presence a steady comfort; and Bea's luminous smile, violin case slung over her shoulder from their teenage years, her light a memory that tugged.

His phone buzzed—Bea's text: "Thinking of you." He left it unanswered, like the others before it, the words weighing like a heavy door he couldn't reopen.

He rose, neck stiff, the gig's roar still thumping, the storm lingering. His hoodie smelled of smoke and sweat, but he pulled it on anyway. Vince's text buzzed—"Verge circling. Meeting soon"—but Dante swiped it away, the promise of arenas drowned by a quieter pull, a need for silence the stage couldn't offer. He stepped into Columbus's dawn, the Scioto River sauntering under a sagging sky. His boots crunched on gravel, leading him to the music hall, a ruin he'd stumbled on a year ago when the spotlight's glare grew too blinding.

The hall stood by the river, a relic of forgotten dreams, its marquee stuttering "CON ERT AL," boarded windows blind to the morning. Ivy clung to its brick like a lover's arms unwilling to surrender. Dante slipped through the rusted side door, hinges groaning in protest, and stepped into a hush that swallowed the world. Dust motes danced in shafts of light piercing the cracked roof. The stage sagged under splintered beams, rows of split seats stretching into shadow like mourners at a funeral. At the center stood a grand piano, chipped mahogany scarred but proud, its strings a mix of snapped wires and those he'd restrung.

He'd found the piano last spring, its broken keys a reflection of the boy he'd buried—the one who'd led worship at sixteen, guitar strumming beside Bea's violin, their voices weaving hymns that felt like flying. The Johnson family had been his hearth: Paul and Maria's steady prayers at dawn, Ben's arm around him, Tessa's quiet smile. Bea had been his friend, her faith a fire he'd borrowed when his faltered, her laughter a melody he hadn't known he loved. As teens, they'd dreamed of music that moved souls, not crowds, but a viral video at seventeen—a dive bar cover gone wild—had slowly pulled him away. Open mics became gigs, gigs became Primal Fire, and the world's call—whiskey, girls, fame—had drowned the hymns, leaving Bea's texts unread, her goodness a still pond reflecting his shame.

Dante sat at the bench, wood creaking under his weight, and let his fingers rest on the keys, cool and uneven. The hall was a sanctuary, its silence not empty but alive, like the pause before a storm. He'd been coming here for months, tools hidden in a duffel, restringing wires when the greenroom's chaos—Jax's boasts, girls' promises, Vince's deals—grew too loud. Each string was a confession, each chord a question: *Who am I now?* He played a single note, thin but clear, cutting through the hush like a star through dusk. Another followed, then a chord, and the music spilled, soft and uneven, a melody born of longing—for Bea, for the boy he'd been, for a faith he'd let slip through his fingers.

The notes wove a memory: Sunday mornings at church, Bea's braid swinging, her violin threading light through his guitar, the congregation's voices rising like a tide. He'd been their prodigy—guitar at ten, leading worship by twelve—Bea at his side, her presence a spark that lit the dark. They'd talked of music as a bridge, a way to touch something bigger. But the stage had called louder, its fire brighter, and he'd drifted, letting her texts— "You okay?"—sit unread, each one a reminder of a world he felt too stained to touch.

The piano's voice deepened, filling the hall with a song that wasn't *Dance of Desire* but something older, solemn, like the psalms they'd sung together—psalms that had first gripped him as a boy. Not just the jubilant ones, but the aching prayers of King David—his uncle's namesake—who sang alone in the hills, harp in hand, the sheep his only audience; who faced a giant with a pebble and rose to a throne; who, caught up the unrelenting tide of power, forgot what mattered and took what wasn't his, sending a loyal man to die.

How far would this swell carry him? Could he let its undertow drag him from those who stood at his side, all for the glitter of more? Somewhere in the back of his mind, another song lingered—half-remembered, etched into his rock-soul from the first time he heard it: *all that glitters is gold*. Maybe he'd misheard it. Maybe he hadn't. Truths buried in the anthems of those he revered, in the lifestyles he chased. Wrapped in all the rock reverie, had those prophetic words been speaking to him all along—not wooing, warning?

A discord cut through, a snapped string's twang, and Dante stopped, breath ragged. The silence rushed back. He stood, pacing the stage, his shadow long in the shifting light. The piano was half-fixed, its keys a work in progress, like his soul—scarred, striving, not yet whole. He thought of Bea, her smile in the photo, her faith, a presence he missed. She was too good, her world too pure, a candle burning steady while he was a wildfire. Burning out.

He knelt by the piano, fingers tracing a crack in the wood, and found a tool he'd left—a small wrench, cold in his palm. He tightened a new string, the wire's thrum a faint promise, but the question lingered: *What am I chasing?*

The hall held him, its ruin a grace he didn't deserve, and he continued to feel the stir—faint yet fierce—like a hand reaching through the dark. His phone buzzed: Bea. "Grandma's asking for you. Come by today?" His breath caught. His heart seemed to move his fingers—"I'm there"—and he rose, the piano's voice still moving him, a quiet vow contending with unseen giants.

Outside, the Scioto's heartbeat returned, welcoming Columbus awakening around him—cars rushing, a dog barking, the river's edge sparkling with dew. The hall's silence lingered like smoke, Bea's words like an ember refusing to die. He wasn't sure what he'd say, but the music had stirred something, a longing not for fame but for truth—for an open door, for the right kind of fire.

Chapter 3: Street Saint

The apartment was brimming with morning chaos, the air thick with burnt toast and coffee's bitter tang. Dante pushed through the door, the hall's echo still ringing, a fragile melody he wasn't ready to share. Octavio "Doc" Ramirez stood at the stove, spatula waving like a conductor's baton. Eggshells littered the counter, a half-empty Corona from last night abandoned on the ledge, and Doc's laughter, rough and alive, cut through.

"Jefe, you're alive" he shouted, his Mexican accent carrying the words with the easy warmth of a kitchen fire. Pouring a mug of coffee and sliding it across, he grinned. "Thought you were pulling a *Freebird* on me." He broke into a mock croon, his accent thick: *"If I leave here tomorrow... gonna fly high... free bird..."*

Dante caught the mug, its heat grounding him, and smirked. "I tried," he said, taking a sip, "but then I saw the fire trucks, smoke pouring out the windows. Figured someone had to save the toast."

Doc barked a laugh, the sound rough but real. Yet his eyes, sharp behind the grin, caught more than the joke—the shadow Dante carried, and beneath it, the faint spark he hadn't seen in a while.

"You got a light in you today, man," Doc said, quieter now. "Where you been?"

"Just air," Dante said, the lie thin, the piano's notes still trembling in his fingers. Doc didn't push, cursing as the toast smoked, and launched into a tale of last night's show—Fred's near-trip over a cable, Jax's flirtation with a purple-haired fan. Dante leaned against the counter, grateful for Doc's chatter, an undertow he didn't have to swim. Octavio was more than a drummer; he was a street saint, his wit a shield, his heart a flame that burned for the broken.

Dante's mind drifted to their first meeting, three summers back, the Scioto sparkling under a July sun. Columbus buzzed with festival energy—fry grease, laughter, music. Dante had been busking near the riverbank, his voice spilling chords before an open case clinking with coins. As dusk settled, he figured he was done, packing up, ready to slip home, when a rhythm erupted like thunder across the crowd, raw and relentless, pulling him to a stop. There was Octavio, nineteen, shirt torn, hammering buckets with sticks, his hands a blur, turning trash into a drum corps as a crowd swelled.

Their eyes locked through the festival frenzy, Octavio's grin a spark as he spotted Dante and, above the stampede, yelled, "Join in, man!" Dante hesitated, then stepped forward, Runkle unleashed, a spontaneous wave of percussive funk peppered with lead runs that danced with Octavio's furious beats, a combustible alchemy igniting the air. A soul-filled brotherhood sparked in that instant, a deep, unspoken bond, their music a shared language. The crowd surged even more, strangers multiplying into a roiling sea, transfixed by the primal magic of their first connection, the raw honesty touching them in places long buried—wounds of loss, flickers of hope, desires unspoken.

Octavio's rhythms carried the professorial precision of Neil Peart on some Rush-lit stage. Dante, amused by his own cleverness, christened him "Doctavian"—a nod to Octavio's surgical brilliance and Peart's moniker, "The Professor." By their second street gig, the name had been whittled down to "Doc," a title the crowds, the papers, and the street chatter all took up. They played

11

for hours, sweat and soul fusing into something greater, Primal Fire born by dusk—its first spark struck in that raw, unpolished moment, a brotherhood set ablaze to burn.

Doc's voice snapped Dante back. The memory of summers at the Johnsons' lakehouse on Lake Diane rose in his mind—Michigan mornings steeped in coffee and mist, evenings lit by music, laughter, and the glow of the dock lights. Cousins fished and skied by day; by night, guitars and violins tangled under the stars, the water carrying their songs. Those gatherings, rich with family and music, had been an anchor in his restless youth, a rhythm still pulsing in his veins, a quiet anchor to his restless heart.

"You gonna drink that or stare at it?" he teased, nodding at the mug. Dante took a sip, the coffee scalding but steadying, and felt the hall's echo shift, not gone but softer, like a song waiting for its verse.

Doc was the product of Abuela Rose, a tiny woman with a voice like a whip who raised him in a dilapidated apartment after his parents vanished into addiction's fog. She taught him rhythm on pots and pans, her hymns becoming his first songs, her prayers a fortress. That day by the river, Dante had seen it—Doc's fire, his grace: a saint in denim who had joined his dream and made it brighter.

The door banged open, Fred's voice booming. "Y'all better not have eaten all the eggs!" He strode in, grocery bag swinging, short-cropped hair damp from a shower, warmth spilling into the room like sunlight.

Jax followed, leather jacket slung over his shoulder, smirk announcing that mischief had entered the room. His gaze carried that restless gleam, always tilted toward the horizon—scanning for the next conquest, whether a woman, a thrill, or a stage to ignite. Nico ghosted in last, pale and quiet, hoodie drawn tight, eyes fixed on some inner secret.

"Too late, lumberjack," Doc shot back, brandishing his spatula like a matador's cape. "Kitchen's closed—kinda like the city's plumbing last time I made you a burrito."

Fred laughed, deep and warm, dumping the bag—milk, cereal, bacon spilling out. "You're a menace, Ramirez," he said, clapping Doc's shoulder. Turning to Dante, "You survive this clown's cooking?"

"Baaarrrely," Dante drawled, the way they always did when *What About Bob?* got quoted—but the hall's melody still held him apart.

Fred was the anchor, who'd sold his car for Dante's first amp and Doc's first drums, loyalty, a steady anchor. Jax was the spark, chasing fame like a sailor fresh off the boat after a red dress. Nico was the phantom, his keys weaving dreams, silence a wall Dante hadn't breached. Together, they were Primal Fire. But today, the hall's pull was stronger than the stage.

Jax flopped onto the couch, thumbs flicking at his phone. "Vince says Verge's ready to drop a number with commas," he announced, eyes gleaming. "No more warehouses. Arenas, boys!"

Fred leaned back, smirking. "Finally. I'll be able to buy you a shirt with sleeves—so we can stop mistaking your arms for chopsticks."

Doc flicked a bottle cap at him. "Could've used one of those last night—" referring to one of his sticks that had gone flying like a javelin into the crowd. He grinned. "Ease up and let Jefe think. He's in the Dante Zone"—shorthand for their regard for the one who made the call at the plate.

Nico leaned against the wall, fingers picking at the frayed hem of his hoodie. Dante wondered what kept him so quiet, what dreams he carried.

"You good, man?" Jax asked. "You're quieter than Fred at an all-you-can-eat salad bar."

Fred didn't look up. "If God wanted me to eat rabbit food, He wouldn't have made cows."

Dante met Doc's gaze and felt the piano's warmth stir in his soul. "I'm in," he said—words meant for the band, not the label.

His phone buzzed again. Bea: "Grandma's excited. Noon?" His throat tightened. The invitation was a bridge to a past he'd buried, to a friend whose light he'd dimmed.

The morning bled into noon, the apartment a swirl of grease and laughter. Fred took over the stove, bacon sizzling, while Jax boasted to fans online, his voice loud with dreams of stadiums. Nico slipped to the fire escape, a cigarette glowing, his silhouette stark against the midday sun. Doc cleaned his kitchen chaos, humming one of Abuela Rose's hymns, his eyes flicking to Dante, seeing the shadow he couldn't hide.

Dante stood, the hall's echo fading but not quite gone. "Gotta run," he said, sidestepping Fred's offer of bacon.

Doc arched an eyebrow, "Tell Bea hi, jefe."

Dante paused—just long enough to meet his friend's quiet mysticism with that familiar half-smirk, half-squint that said, *How the hell do you always know?* Then he turned and left, the band's chatter dissolving behind him as he stepped into the low buzz of Columbus.

The Scioto rumbled gently along at his side, a soft counterpoint to his quickening heartbeat, guiding him toward the retirement home—a low, weathered brick building with wilted roses unfurling at the edges.

Bea waited in the lobby, violin case at her feet, her dark hair loose, her smile soft but searching. "Dante," she said, her voice a

14

melody, stepping close, her presence a warmth he hadn't felt in years. "You came."

"Couldn't miss Grandma," he said, throat tight. Her eyes wistful, but her smile held. "She's a fighter," she said, leading him down a hall, her steps steady but light.

They reached a small room, photos lining the walls—Bea as a child, her mother's smile, a violin in every frame. Grandma Caldwell sat by the window, frail but fierce, her white hair a halo, her eyes sparkling with a mischief that mirrored Bea's, tempered by decades. "Beatrice!" she said, voice crackling with warmth. "And the rockstar. About time you showed up."

Dante grinned, the tension easing, and sat beside her, Bea's laughter lifting the room. "Heard you're the real star around here," he teased, winking, and Grandma's laughter filled the space. "Don't flatter an old lady," she said, but her gaze pinned him, seeing past the stage. "You've got fire, Dante. Don't let it burn you out."

Her words landed, heavy with truth, and Dante felt Bea's eyes, her presence already holding something within him he didn't know needed to be held until just then. They talked—Grandma's tales of jazz clubs in the '60s, Bea's childhood practicing scales under her mother's watchful eye, music that carried them through loss. Dante listened, the rockstar fading, the boy who'd sung hymns with Bea returning, if only for a moment.

Grandma's eyes locked on his, steady as bedrock, seeing straight through but holding him there like she was in no hurry to let go. In them, he felt the grandmother he'd never met—weathered by storms, lit with the quiet flame of someone who'd walked through fire and come out tempered, not burned. Her gaze didn't just read him; it welcomed him, as if to say he belonged here. "I see your grandma in you, Dante," she said, her hand trembling on his. "She learned young what you're finding now—that the truths worth keeping are forged in the storm. You only own them when you know Who owns you."

Dante's breath halted, a lump rising in his throat before he even knew it was there, a single tear pricking at the corner of his eye. Beside him, Bea's cheeks flushed, her eyes wide with shared emotion. Grandma's smile turned sly as she nodded toward Bea. Then her eyes focused—piercing, certain—catching him off guard. "You love her, don't you?" she said, voice low but sure.

Dante froze, heart racing, Bea's gaze locking with his, warm and searching. He didn't answer, Grandma's quiet chuckle breaking the silence. "Don't run, boy," she said. "Love like that's rare." Bea laughed, breaking the moment, but her piercing look held his, a question unspoken, a spark that warmed the room.

They left, Bea's hand brushing his as they walked the hall, the Scioto's gentle rustle through a window. "She sees too much," Bea said, her smile teasing but warm. "But she's right about you. You're carrying something, Dante. What is it?"

He stopped, the city's bustle fading into a hush, as if the streets themselves were holding their breath. "It's like… you remember when we played together that night in the park?" His voice softened, eyes flicking toward her as if the memory was a fragile thing he didn't want to break. "No big crowds. No spotlights. Just the music—raw and alive—like we were caught up in something bigger than us. It was… right."

He exhaled, looking away, the words reluctant at first, like they had to be pried out of him. "But after that… it's like I've been walking a line. Every door swinging open, like God Himself drew it. And I believed it. I still want to." His voice cracked, then steadied, softer now. "But looking back… I wonder if something else slipped in—looked like the line, but just a degree off. You don't feel that at first. Not until one day it hits you here—" he tapped his chest, his hand lingering there, fingers curling tight as if holding something broken. "—and you look up, and you're miles from where you thought you were headed."

Silence pooled between them. His eyes dropped to the ground, words slowing, almost swallowed. "I don't know… am I really that far gone? And if I could go back… would I?"

A lump caught in his throat. Bea didn't answer, her gaze fixed on him the way a mountain might watch a lost traveler. She saw the distance wasn't just about them. It was something deeper, something he'd have to face alone. But somewhere in her stillness, in the unblinking steadiness of her eyes, was the faintest glimmer—like a star that only appears when you're far enough from the city lights to see it.

"The stage, the crowds—it's all I've got," Dante continued, eyes fixed somewhere past her shoulder. "But I know it's not enough."

Bea tilted her head, searching his face. "It never is, is it?" she said quietly. She had so much more to say, but held her words close.

He swallowed hard. "You… you're too good for me."

Her brow creased, not with pity but with something steadier. "I'm not perfect, Dante. Dad's got me playing for his world, not mine."

He almost looked away, but her gaze held him—steady, unflinching—like she'd been keeping that place for him all along. "Your music…" She paused, letting the words breathe, her eyes never leaving his. "You… are so honest." She said it like it was a truth he'd forgotten, one she was determined not to let slip away. "That's why I'm still here. Why I text."

Her smile was faint, but her eyes carried something heavier—something he felt before he could name. It wasn't anger. It was the kind of ache that belonged to someone whose love had been betrayed, who listened to every song even though wrapped in another woman's perfume, and chose to stay anyway. Not to excuse it, not to pretend it didn't matter, but because she could see past it. Because she saw the man in it all the world would never see.

She didn't look away, and in that stillness he felt a shift—like she was inviting him to stand in the truth without flinching. "I don't have to agree with all of it," she said finally. "And I certainly don't have to like it." Pain in her words hung there, soft in tone but weighted in meaning, and he knew she wasn't just talking about his set list. There was no accusation, but there was loss—loss she would not lay at his feet, even as it pulsed between them.

"I just know," she went on, "there's more in you than the noise, the stage, your adoring fans…." She pressed her hand to his chest—tender, steady, like a prayer. "But real fire—the kind that never burns out. And I think the One who put it there… He's not finished with you yet."

Her words should have felt like grace—and in part they did. But something else rose with them, sharp and uninvited: the sting of betrayal. She saw too clearly what he had worked so hard to bury, even from himself. And beneath it, a deeper ache: the quiet, disarming awareness that she was right. For a moment, a story flickered—of a king, drunk with power, taking what was not his. He'd had his Bathshebas. But Bea… Bea was Uriah-faithful, steady and true, even when she could see the battlefield for what it was. The thought lingered, unwelcome, heavy. Would he betray her, too?

He felt it then—the stage roaring in his blood, but her presence burning against it, a flame that refused to waver. For a breath, he let himself rest there, caught in her light, the pull of something truer rising around him.

Then the current shifted. From the deep, unseen places. Shapes slid upward, curling like tentacles from a black sea. They came as they always did: sudden, relentless, wrapping tight. They wore the faces of a hundred little moments—doors nudged open because they seemed harmless and anonymous. Each one part of a shimmering line he'd followed so long it felt like destiny. A

18

line that gleamed with promise but bent, almost imperceptibly, from the one he'd known as a boy.

She seemed to sense it—the faint shadow crossing his eyes, the way something unseen brushed past him, tugging. Her eyes held him with the kind of love older than words, the kind that makes you want to turn away before it undoes you. "You're not as alone as you think," she said, her voice low, deliberate. "Something greater is guiding you… even if you can't see it yet. Even if another voice is fighting to make sure you don't."

Her words stung, stirring memories of Paul's prayers, Maria's hymns, a faith he thought had flickered out. He wanted to believe her, but the rockstar life had become louder. "I'm trying," he said, voice breaking. She squeezed his arm, her touch a promise.

"Keep trying," she said, her smile soft but reassuring. "Come to Dad's fundraiser Saturday night? Play for them. Play for me."

Drawn into the warmth of her tide, Dante nodded. Against the pull of the shadow, it felt almost like a vow—the closest he'd come in years. A decision you make. Regardless of what you feel. Regardless of what makes sense. Regardless of what you think you can do.

They parted, the river's whisper trailing him back, the ache in his heart an ember longing for air.

Chapter 4: The Girl and the Strings

The river's whisper was faint, its surface glowing with the amber hush of evening as Dante slipped through the music hall's rusted side door, the city's clamor softened to a low drone, as though even the streets were catching their breath. The light hesitated, unsure whether to linger or leave. The air inside was cooler now, touched with the quiet solemnity of a day letting go. The hall had become a companion. A ruin of forgotten promises—boarded windows blind to the river's glow, cracked beams sagging like old bones, dust eddies curling through fading light that slanted down from fractured rafters. For months, even more than a companion, it had been his refuge, a place where the stage's roar—crowds screaming, girls clinging, whiskey blurring into dawn—fell silent.

The grand piano at its heart, once a wreck of snapped strings and chipped keys, was nearly whole, the last wire drawn taut under a sliver of moon, as if the heavens bore silent witness to something being remade. Dante's fingers were raw from the labor, like truths unearthed—fragments he had carried quietly until the day before.

He sat at the bench, wood complaining, and let his hands hover over the keys, their polished edges a stark contrast to the hall's decay. The piano was a mirror, scarred but singing, a testament to stolen hours when the rockstar life grew too heavy. Yesterday's visit with Bea hadn't just stirred something—it had unsettled him. Her smile still lingered, Grandma Caldwell's sly nudge replaying like a riff he couldn't shake. That fundraiser invite felt less like a polite ask and more like a door swinging open, and he wasn't sure what waited on the other side. The thought of stepping into her world again—where hymns rose like breath and faith held its ground—pulled at something in him that the stage could never reach.

He played a single note, clear and resounding, piercing the silence like a spark in the dark. Another followed, then a chord, and the music spilled, untamed and unrelenting, a torrent of grief and longing. The world's weight pressed in—Jax's hunger for fame, Vince's endless calls, the girls whose names blurred into smoke—and Dante let it pour through his fingers, the piano's voice a cry he couldn't speak. He played for Bea, for the Johnson family's Sunday mornings, for Grandpa Michael's unyielding prayers, each note a mystery laid bare, each melody a hope. The hall listened, its secrets swaying, its silence cradling him like a current pulling toward shore.

Outside, following a particularly intense rehearsal, Bea walked the river's edge, her violin case a steady weight, her heart heavy with her father's demands—perfect notes, perfect poise, a life polished to please his conservatory's donors. Dr. Caldwell's voice echoed in her mind, crisp and unyielding: "Beatrice, you're our star. Don't falter." She'd played his game, her violin a tool for his ambition, but the music felt shallow, a cage around the fire she'd once shared with Dante. A sound stopped her—a piano, fierce and haunting, spilling from the music hall's boarded walls. She knew the place, the relic her father's gala was set to honor tomorrow night, a flailing entity drowning in the sea of time's passage slated for resuscitation.

The thought summoned to her mind Victor Hugo's *Les Misérables*, where Jean Valjean envisions himself as a man overboard in the middle of the ocean, watching the ship move on without him, his strength ebbing until staying above the water becomes battle. Bea felt the same exhaustion: captive to ambitions not her own, at the mercy of currents she had not chosen, and yet drawn toward the terrifying clarity that if she were to live—truly live—something in her would have to die.

Her breath quickened as she followed the sound, drawn by something deeper than memory, as if her soul recognized its song before her mind did. The front doors were locked, the windows blind, but the music grew louder, guiding her to the rusted side door, hanging loose like an open wound. She pushed it open, hinges groaning, and stepped into the hall's hush, the piano's voice a surge that carried her forward. Dust spiraled in the golden light, the stage a splintered ruin, and there—at the battered piano—was Dante: dark curls damp with sweat, shoulders bowed, hands moving with an unbridled passion that seemed to set the shadows dancing.

Her chest tightened, her eyes welling with recognition—not of his face, but his soul, the music a language they'd shared since youth. Yesterday's words still lingered between them, unspoken now but alive, the kind that change the air when two people breathe it. It was Dante—her friend, the boy she'd loved in a girl's quiet way, who'd vanished into fame's blaze but never left her heart. She stood in the twilight, transfixed by his playing, the raw ache of his notes, and wanted to leave, to let him have this solitude. But her hands betrayed her, opening her violin case with a soft click, the bow trembling as she drew it across the strings.

The first note was a whisper, timid against his storm, but it grew, bold and clear, weaving into his melody like a hand slipping into another's. Dante's fingers faltered, his head lifting, the piano pausing as the violin's song filled the hall, a rising voice in the quiet. He turned, and their eyes met—his wide with shock, hers shimmering with tears, a sea of unsaid words passing like rapids. It was more than sound—it was the conversation they hadn't finished yesterday, the language they'd always shared when words fell short. He knew her sound, her soul, as she knew his, and his hands returned to the keys, the piano answering her violin, their music a dance of light and shadow, a harmony that felt like coming home.

They played, not for the hall, not for the world, but for each other, their notes entwining in a moment that transcended time.

22

Dante's heart unfurled, his unspoken love for her—deep, fierce, too vast for words—pouring through the keys, healing wounds he couldn't name. Bea's violin soared, her longing for him—hesitant, then fearless—lifting them both, their music a unity woven by something greater, a presence they felt but didn't speak, like a current pulling toward eternity. The hall was alive, its dust moving like incense, its reverberation a song that spoke of redemption.

The music stretched, boundless, each movement a thread binding their souls, restoring what time had fractured. Dante saw her at sixteen, her braid swinging, her faith a beacon he'd followed. Bea saw him even more now, not just his depths, but his fire burning true, raw and radiant. It was more than friendship, a glimpse of something deeper, a healing that reached into their core, lifted by a force beyond themselves. The notes faded, the final chord hanging like a star, and the hall fell silent, its hush heavier now, saturated with what had passed.

Dante's hands rested on the keys, Bea's bow lowered, and they looked at each other, breathless, eyes wet, hearts laid bare. Neither spoke, the silence a vessel for what they'd shared, until Bea, her voice soft as dawn, said, "So… there's that."

Dante laughed, a sound wild and free, like a chain breaking, and nodded, his throat too tight for words. They didn't need to speak of love or pasts—the music had spoken, opening a horizon of friendship, of truth, a connection that could carry them forward. They sat on the stage, the river's rustle seeping through the walls, and Dante felt whole.

Bea broke the quiet, her smile teasing but warm. "You're still you, Dante. Under all the lights, the crowds. I hear it." She tapped her violin case, her eyes steady, but sensing his reluctance. "Play with me tomorrow. Not for Dad, not for them—for us."

He met her gaze, the piano's echo mingling with her light, and nodded. "For us," he said, the words a vow, the hall's grace binding them. They stood and walked the Scioto's banks, the city hushed around them. Bea spoke of simple things—her grandmother's stories, the river's quiet beauty—her presence a balm to Dante's storm. He listened, and when she turned to him, her eyes clear, she said, "You don't have to be what they want, Dante. Just be you."

Her words landed and he nodded, the hall's music, her invitation, a promise he couldn't break. They parted at the river's bend, Bea's smile a warmth that lingered. Dante walked back to the apartment, the Scioto's whisper a quiet call, Vince's texts— "Verge's waiting"—unanswered on his phone. The fundraiser loomed, a stage not his own, but Bea's faith, their duet, carried him forward, a path he didn't understand but couldn't deny.

Back in the apartment, Doc was sprawled on the couch, turning his drumsticks on a table, his grin sly. "Saw Bea's glow, jefe," he said, eyes twinkling. "You playing for her tomorrow?"

Dante smirked, dodging the jab. "Just helping a friend," he said, but Doc's laugh followed him to his room, the piano's melody still ringing.

Chapter 5: Primal Fire

The Caldwell house loomed on Columbus's west side, a fortress of wealth with marble steps gleaming under dusk's violet glow. Chandeliers cast golden light through tall windows, their shimmer bouncing off polished floors where professors, donors, and suits mingled. Dante stood at the edge of the foyer, jeans and faded hoodie out of place among tailored jackets, his guitar case a quiet rebellion against the room's sheen. The air smelled of lavender and money, a world far from the Scioto's muddy banks, the music hall's cobwebs, or the warehouse's sweat-soaked chaos.

Bea stood on a small stage at the room's heart, her violin tucked under her chin, her dark hair pinned in a loose bun, her navy dress catching the light like a still lake. Dr. Caldwell, silver-haired and crisp in a tailored suit, addressed the crowd, his voice a proclamation of his conservatory's prestige, his daughter's brilliance. "Beatrice is our future," he said, his smile tight, his eyes flicking to her with a mix of pride and command. The guests nodded, their applause polite, their faces masks of expectation. Bea's bow raised, but her fingers trembled; for one shaming instant she thought of lowering the instrument, of walking away—letting the donors keep their sterile silence. *Maybe I'm not enough for this,* the thought hissed. Her breath faltered, eyes wet, before she forced the bow steady. Notes came, Vivaldi flowing like water over stone, but Dante saw the strain in her shoulders, the flicker in her eyes—ornate, ordered bars of her father's making, dimming the fire he knew was there.

He'd almost stayed away, the hall's duet still resounding in his soul, Bea too bright for the shadow he carried. But her words by the river—"Play for us"—had been a solemn pledge. The apartment had been quiet when he left, Doc's knowing grin the only send-off, Jax and Fred out chasing gigs, Nico lost in his own world. Vince's texts—"Verge's ready"—sat unanswered, the lure of arenas hovering like a phantom over Bea's melody.

Now, standing in this gilded room, Dante felt the distance between their worlds, his calloused fingers twitching, the piano in the corner a beacon he wasn't sure he could reach. As Bea's last note lingered, the applause was crisp, practiced, like silverware clicking against china. Her poise flawless, her cheeks radiant from the glow of admiration. Dr. Caldwell beamed, his jaw tight, his pride satisfied.

Then she turned. "I'd like you to meet my friend," she said, her voice unwavering. "Dante Johnson."

Heads swiveled. The air shifted. A murmur rippled—curiosity laced with skepticism. Dante felt the weight of it, a hundred eyes appraising him, pinning him in place. His throat tightened.

This wasn't the hall. This wasn't the cracked plaster and aching shadows where music rose unbidden, raw and true. This was marble and chandeliers, a room built for perfection. And he wasn't perfect.

His boots scuffed the polished floor as he moved toward the grand piano, each step wrong, too heavy, too loud in the hush. He hesitated, glancing at Bea. She smiled, steady, urging him forward. For her, he went.

He sat, the grand piano gleaming black beneath the sterile gaze of portraits locked in their frames, its polished surface catching the light like a mirror meant to expose him. His reflection looked wrong—awkward, out of place, a stray note in a score too perfect. The hush pressed down, a room of silks and polished shoes waiting to measure him against their scales.

26

Why did he play? The question crowded in, louder than the silence, an indictment he felt in their eyes. He'd never played for rooms like this. His music had never lived in crystal and marble. It had always belonged to the streets, to the raw air, to the open. To the places where the broken dared to listen.

And the thought tore him open—because here, now, he could feel it threatened, that primal spark, the reason he'd ever played at all.

For a moment, he closed his eyes. And the memory came.

The busking corner in Columbus. At sixteen, to play in public was more than sharing a song—it was laying himself bare, a referendum on his worth. Every chord carried the ache of a question: *Am I enough? Will they care?* The streets bustled, indifferent, the crowd a river streaming past. Nine out of ten glances slid off him like rain on stone. The silence stung more than heckling; it measured him. Too rarely, coins clinked into his case—thin offerings that felt more like pity than belief. He remembered the heaviness of those walks home, calloused fingers empty, chest hollow, wondering if he was deluded, chasing a dream already out of reach. In his head he could almost hear Simon Cowell's British sneer: *"That was absolutely pathetic. Don't give up your day job."*

And then one day—*him*. The old man on the bench, across the street. At first Dante thought little of it—just someone catching his breath before moving on. But as songs rose and fell, crowds spilling past in their hurried tides, the man remained. Song after song, still there. Not watching in idle curiosity, but fixed, his look cutting across the traffic, across the noise, straight into Dante. There was something in his countenance—haggard and worn, yet bearing a quiet gravity—that made Dante feel read, as if his own doubts and longings were being silently understood.

When the last notes faded and Dante began to pack up, the man still hadn't moved. Something in him felt the pull, as if an aura— almost sacred—had gathered around this unlikely throne. The old man's eyes—weathered, unblinking—held him fast. Then he spoke, his voice low and rough, like gravel underfoot, yet carrying an authority that made the words impossible to brush aside:

"Let me see that thing."

Reluctant but compelled, Dante opened the case, lifted out Runkle, and set it in the man's hands. He braced for clumsy fumbling, a plucked string or two—but the man held it like a relic, fingers brushing the grain, the scars, the frets, with the tenderness of someone reunited with a long-lost love. He closed his eyes, drew in a deep breath, and touched a single string. Then another. The sound was rough, nearly broken, yet carried a startling familiarity. A strum followed—halting at first, then steady, then swelling into rhythm—raw, unvarnished, but alive.

And then a song rose. Not trained, not smooth, but a cry from the depths—half lament, half hymn. Words stumbled out, jagged and imperfect, but hauntingly real: of love lost and found, hunger and exile, fire smoldering under ash yet still burning. A mourning song, yes, but more than that—something soul-deep, as though creation itself bent closer to listen. He sang not to the crowd, not even to Dante, but from beneath them both, from a place no polish could touch.

Dante felt it before he understood it: something inside him splitting open, something named at last. This wasn't performance—it was presence. Not metaphor but heat, a flame rising through him, searing, purifying. Baptism, not by water but by fire. He trembled, not because the man was great, but because the song was real—more real than coins in the case, more real than the applause he had once craved.

From that moment, music changed. His soul changed. Or rather, awakened. It wasn't about applause, or the market's measuring sticks. It was about the fire in his bones—about truth, about giving voice to what no wall, no mask, no stage could contain. The man disappeared into the crowd, never seen again, but the

28

flame he struck burned on. And when Dante and the others one day needed a name, there was never a question what it had to be.

Primal Fire.

Now, in this regal room, with pearls and pomposity sneering in silence, he thought of that man. Of the gift he had been given. Of Bea, standing there, asking him to bring it.

All at once he felt himself the old man, that same heart beating now within his own. He looked out across the room and saw more than polished facades—past collars and pearls, into the hidden aches beneath, the quiet captivity no one dared name. From that depth the song began to rise, unbidden, pressing against him until he could not hold it back. He bowed his head, closed his eyes, drew a long breath, and struck a chord—simple, low, aching. The sound lingered, hanging like the calm before a storm. He let it move, let it swell, let it cry. And then, circling like storm clouds, the words came—breaking loose, not rehearsed, but outpoured.

Here I am, wondering what you'd say,
If I opened my heart—would you turn away?
Would you see the cracks where the light breaks through,
Where the prayers we whisper still carry truth,
And call us to rise, to begin anew?

Caged wings, caged wings,
Meant for the sky, yet bound by strings.
Caged wings, caged wings,
Set me free—
From caged wings.

His voice cracked, untrained, but it carried with a fierceness of the first light on the first dawn. The chords rose, piano and voice entwined in something more than music.

I see your faces polished, calm, composed,
But I hear the silence in the words you've closed.

Would you bare the scars that you try to hide,
Let the truth come rushing from the other side,
To feel, to breathe, to live, to fly?

Caged wings, caged wings,
Meant for the sky, yet bound by strings.
Caged wings, caged wings,
Set us free—
From caged wings.
From caged wings.
From caged wings.
Set us free.

It was a cry, a tearing open. And it disarmed. Whispers stilled. A woman dabbed her eyes. A man shifted, uncomfortable, as though the song had reached somewhere he'd sealed away.

It wasn't polished. It wasn't classical. It was truth. And it was out of place.

When the final note faded, silence followed—not the reverent kind, but a silence too tight, too self-conscious, as though the room wasn't sure what had just happened or how to hold it.

Dante rose, chest heavy. "I'm sorry," he said, low, turning to Bea. "I… I shouldn't have…."

Bea's hands had flown to her mouth, pressed together like a prayer. Tears slid down her cheeks, catching light like stars trembling into being. For so long she had played to the piper's tune—measured, precise, gilded notes that won applause but kept her caged. And here, in a few unpolished words and chords, in one sacred moment, Dante had stepped into her world—the world of carefully curated control—and shaken it to its core.

She glanced across the room through her tears and saw it: women fighting sobs, undone in spite of themselves; men red faced, stiff in their collars, jaws clenched against something they could not master. The cage was trembling, its bars exposed. This is what she felt—that first breath of air beyond the bars. What he had risked, what he had laid bare, had not only freed him; it had touched her—the first spark of friendship, the ache of silent years, the reunion in Grandma Caldwell's knowing grin, the duet in the broken auditorium, and now this night veiled in the promise of restoration. It was too precise to be chance; some greater hand was moving, weaving their steps toward a purpose neither could yet name. She saw it all, and she saw him—not the rockstar, not the boy, but a man who had entered her cage and broken it open. Who didn't even know what he had done. For the first time, she felt the hope of being free.

His gaze caught hers, and from the depths of her soul the words welled up unbidden, pressed to her lips though no sound escaped: *I love you.*

Dante felt them, as surely as if they had been spoken aloud. They pierced him with a purity so unguarded it left him vacated of all else. For a heartbeat he longed to answer, to return what surged in him with equal abandon. But the shadow still clung—shame whispering *unworthy, dirty, chained.* And in the hollow of that moment, he knew: the song had not been for them. *Caged wings*—it was his own plea. His own cry. And he wasn't yet sure if it could be otherwise.

A woman stepped forward. Gray hair swept elegantly, presence commanding. Eleanor Voss. Her eyes were wet, but her voice was steady.

"That," she said, her words cutting through the chatter, "was real. You're not what they think. Keep playing." She pressed a card into Dante's hand. Then she was gone, the ripple of her presence lingering.

Dr. Caldwell was quick to step in, his smile tight, his voice tremulous with embarrassment. "Thank you, Mr. Johnson. And now, ladies and gentlemen, let us return to why we're gathered here tonight—to restore this hall to its rightful grandeur." His

31

words swept like a broom, redirecting, smothering, as if nothing unscripted had just occurred.

Bea touched Dante's arm gently, tears still adorning her eyes. A thousand unspoken words pressed between them, too heavy to release. When she tried to speak, it was as if breaking the seal would loose a flood. Her voice faltered, caught in fragments: "That… you…" She steadied herself, drew a breath, and managed, "Here…" Then, gathering what composure she could, she tilted her head toward the door. "Out there?"

Dante only nodded, the weight of it clear, and followed.

The night air was cool against their skin, the river a quiet hymn under the starlit sky. Bea's hand in his was warm, steady, a tether against the shadows. She slowed, turning to face him, her eyes holding his. In that stillness, she seemed to see his battle, what was going on in his depths, the parts won and those yet under captivity. She understood the inevitable road stretching ahead— the hands trying to pull him away. Yet in her gaze was a certainty. "What just happened… this… you… don't ever forget it. This is real," she said, her voice barely above the river's murmur. "The fire you were made for. Wherever you go, whatever tries to claim you… this remains."

He nodded, the weight of her words settling deep—how she'd seen him, named him, in a way no one had. It startled him, how right she was, and how much the past three days had felt like someone—or something—was threading his path on purpose. But even as that thought rose, the shadow slid in, smooth and sure, velvet promises curling around his resolve. The contract waited, unspent ink already feeling like iron, yet the stage's blaze beckoned. "I have to go," he said at last, voice raw, torn between two worlds. "The tour—Vegas, New York. It's everything we've worked for."

Bea's eyes darkened, but she didn't stop him, her faith a compass that didn't waver. "You're not alone," she said, her voice steady. "Even when you run."

He left, the river's sigh fading behind him. The apartment was empty, the band out, and Dante sat on the fire escape, his phone buzzing with Vince's texts—"Verge's ready. Sign tomorrow"— and Bea's last message: "I'm praying for you." He didn't reply.

Chapter 6: Shadows of the Stage

Verge Records' glass tower pierced the Columbus sky, its sterile gleam a mockery of the crumbling brick that still sheltered the old music hall. Dante sank into a leather chair, the air thick with cologne and calculation. His heel tapped an uneven rhythm against the polished floor, a nervous drumbeat the executives pretended not to hear.

Lucian Vega, the label's agent, leaned across the mahogany desk, his grin smooth as velvet—promising stardom with effortless charm. As Dante glanced around the room, the faces on the walls rose to meet him—rock gods immortalized, stoking the hunger that had grown since his first viral spark, urging: *Welcome to the wall.*

Lucian's piercing eyes locked on Dante's. "Gentlemen," he purred, spreading contracts like a dealer's cards, "welcome to the big time. *Dance of Desire* is a phenomenon. Sign here, and we'll shape your sound, your style, your story—arenas, global tours, a number with commas."

Jax leaned forward, leather jacket creaking, eyes hungry as a wolf's. "This is it, boys," he said, pen already in hand. Fred exhaled, his fingers drumming the table, betraying nerves he couldn't name. Nico sat silent, pale, hoodie drawn tight, his nod barely a surrender. Doc hesitated, gaze fixed on Dante—a plea unspoken. Dante heard Bea's words—*You're more than this*—but Lucian's vision pressed harder, drowning them out.

The label draped promises—chart-topping singles, world tours, their faces on every magazine rack. But the fine print bled compromise. Lyrics returned marked in red, reshaped to echo whatever chorus the market craved. Stage clothes arrived on rolling racks, tagged with someone else's idea of who they were. Cameras clicked in rehearsed angles, interview cards slid across tables with the right answers already underlined.

Somewhere in the back of his mind, Dante thought of Robert Johnson at the crossroads—the shared last name they once laughed about, now feeling real, whispering the bargain before him. In the undertow Clapton's voice rose, gravel and prayer entwined:

I went down to the crossroads,
Fell down on my knees,
Asked the Lord above for mercy,
"Save me, if you please!"

The words clung like smoke, heavy with all Clapton had borne—the fame and brilliance, but also the crash into addiction, the ache of loss, grief too burdensome to name. That was the cost, written not in contracts but in scars. Dante stared at the fruit laid before him, whispering that he could be different. *After all, it's just a contract. You can walk away at any time.*

Lucian beckoned again. "You're the heart, Dante. Primal Fire's soul. Sign, and we'll make you icons." The words fanned the flame, but something else pressed back—lives shrink-wrapped for sale, their truth smothered under Verge's gleam.

Feeling the gravity of it, the inevitability, Nico exhaled, and barely audible, a word came out more sigh than sound. "Final."

The others let it pass. But Dante paused. There was something in the way Nico said it—not dramatic, but heavy, resigned. It felt like a toll. The word lingered—faint as breath, deep as a bell. *Final.*

For a moment it cut through the dazzle—a warning. Dante's breath seized, his hand hovering over the pen, the weight of the word like a hand on his shoulder, urging him to turn back. But the walls seemed to close in: the rock gods staring down, inviting him forward.

The grip tightened, slow and certain, like chains he hadn't noticed until they cinched shut. Dante took the pen and signed, the ink binding him to Lucian's machine. The room erupted— Lucian's grin intensifying, Jax whooping, Fred's clap too slow, too heavy, unease hidden under noise. Dante's heart was stone. The music hall's piano turned silent. He could almost hear his own voice folding into Clapton's lament: *Believe I am sinking down.*

That night, the band celebrated at a rooftop club, Columbus's lights, a sea of stars below, champagne fizzing in flutes, laughter inebrial and reckless. Girls closed in, their touches fleeting but relentless. Jax dove in, a king in his element, while Fred laughed too loud, swayed by the buzz, his loyalty steady but dulled. Nico slipped to the balcony, his outline cut against the skyline, cigarette burning like a solitary watchlight. Doc stayed near Dante, sipping his beer, eyes steady, seeing the shadow no stage light could burn away.

"You feel it, don't you, jefe?" he said, voice low, cutting through the din. "That ink. It didn't just leave its mark on paper."

Dante just stared, words snagging in his throat, and drained his whiskey, clinging to its burn for comfort. Then something shifted—an almost imperceptible shadow crossing his face. He straightened, voice rising, louder now, as if sheer volume could smother the doubt. His hands carved the air as he spoke, the bearing of a man newly crowned, wielding the command of one who believed he could decide what was true.

"This is what we were made for. What we've worked for. From that first jam. It's what we've dreamed about."

He grinned, eyes bright, the words tumbling faster, bolder, as though saying them made them true. "Yeah, we signed, but we're still in control."

Then he paused, a spark of sobriety marked by a grimace, humor rushing in to cover the weight.

"No way in hell I'm wearing spandex... or whatever else they want me to wear."

Doc chuckled, low and warm, shaking his head like an older brother who'd heard this bravado before. But the laugh faded quickly, his eyes locking on Dante's with a clarity that stripped the noise away. He saw past the swagger, past the smirk, past the shadow, straight into the cavern where the ache lived.

"It's not too late," Doc said, quiet but unyielding. "You can still choose."

But Dante shook his head, the shadow pressing in, Lucian's chain tugging even in his absence. "It's done," he said, turning away from Doc's gaze.

The tour began—Chicago's United Center first, then Detroit's Fox Theatre, New York's Madison Square Garden—each city a blur of neon and screams, each concert a fire that burned hotter. The stage was a cage, the shadow a roar, the crowds swelling, ten thousand, twenty, their worship, a drug that fed the rockstar but was starving the man. Backstage, the parties blurred— champagne, laughter, pills slipped into his hand by dealers with snake smiles. Dante took them, the bitter edge numbing the ache, blurring memory of Bea's glow, Doc's warnings, the hall's grace.

Bea's texts came less often now—*Just thinking of you... no need to reply... I'm here if you need me*—but he never answered, each silence another brick in the wall. The phrase jabbed at him like a taunt, as if the culture had already written his confession into its soundtrack, echoing Pink Floyd's anthem of isolation. His shame pressed close, but whenever it threatened to break him, a darker whisper smothered it—*Catholic guilt*, it sneered, as though naming it stripped it of weight. Still, she came in dreams: Bea with her violin, a flame fierce enough to burn through ash, her music tearing cracks in the barricade. But morning always betrayed him. The emptiness rushed back, and the stage's roar thundered over her memory, drowning it before it could reach him.

In a Philly hotel, the night was a bruise, the city a faint buzz through cracked windows. Dante sat alone, a bottle empty, the shadow louder now—*You're broken, dirty, beyond saving.* He thought of the music hall, its piano silent, its grace unreachable. He thought of Bea, her violin, her persistent heart and wept, the tears hot, the whiskey a fire that didn't warm.

Sleep came, a thief, and dragged him into a dream that wasn't a dream but a descent. The world was ash and thorns, a forest of twisted shadows, the air thick with screams not human. *Descent Into Darkness* played—not his voice, but a chorus of whispers, the lyrics a blade:

The signs were there, the truth was spoken,
But lies were fed and bonds were broken…

Lucian stood at a cliff's edge, his grin too wide, his eyes too deep, offering a crown of flames. "You're mine," he said, and the ground crumbled, a void below pulsing with eyes—red, unblinking, hungry. Dante's sins—girls, pride, betrayal—spilled like blood, and he screamed, the sound swallowed by the dark.

Descent into the fire, feel the grip of Hell's desire,
The darkness waits, it's calling you,
And every word, it's been told, it's true.

He woke gasping, the hotel room cold, the bottle on the floor, the dream clinging like a charred wraith, whispering louder than ever: *beyond redemption.* His phone buzzed. The glow on the nightstand cut through the dark, and there it was—Bea's text: *Grandma's dying. Please come.* The words hit harder than the dream, more piercing than the pills, a cry from the one tether he had left. For a beat he saw her face, saw the woman who had named his depths and called him out, saw the old smile that still haunted his marrow.

And then the shadow pressed in. He told himself he couldn't go, not now, not with the tour in motion, not with everything he'd signed binding him to the machine. Contracts, schedules, stages—excuses rose like scaffolding around him, but he knew they were only that: excuses. The truer weight was darker—the shame, the guilt, the gnawing sense that if he showed up, he'd be exposed for what he'd become. He didn't type a reply. Didn't even open the message again. His silence was its own verdict, another brick in the wall. He lay back, staring at the ceiling as if it might crack with the pressure. Bea's words burned in his hand, her plea echoing in his heart, but his body stayed pinned, his will shackled. The guilt should have driven him to her, but instead it hollowed him further, a heaviness that kept him still. He closed his eyes, letting the roar of the shadow drown out her voice, telling himself it was too late already.

He didn't go. The tour rolled on—city after city, the stage his cage, the shadow stoking his roar. What chased him wasn't fame or failure, but something older, heavier, a truth he wasn't ready to face. He felt it closing in, breath hot at his back, and so he ran.

Chapter 7: The Breaking Point

The tour was a crucible, each city dragging Dante deeper. At Red Rocks, mountains loomed like ancient judges, crags catching starlight as Primal Fire played to ten thousand. *Dance of Desire* was a jagged cry, shaking the stone, the crowd's screams a wave. Fred's bass beat, strained, his eyes on Dante's trembling hands, remembering the night he sold his car for the band—after his brother died in a wreck, a wound that drove his loyalty. Doc's drums faltered, worry breaking their gallop, his rosary tattoo glinting with Abuela's prayers. Jax's guitar snarled, chasing stadiums, blind to the fracture, his hunger born in a childhood of empty cupboards, strumming a borrowed guitar to escape poverty's bite. Nico's keys wove dissonance, mirroring Dante's soul, his silence heavy with unspoken grief. Their gazes met, the band's brotherhood fraying.

Backstage, smoke and liquor choked the air. Jax laughed with a promoter while Fred lingered near Doc, an unspoken question marking his countenance. Nico sketched in a corner, pencil carving a stage aflame. Doc gripped Dante's shoulder. "Jefe, you're slipping," he said, voice fierce. "Bea's broken. Her grandma's gone. You didn't show."

Dante's chest seized, Bea's text—*Grandma's dying. Please come*—still stinging from weeks ago in Philly. Silence had built a wall, brick upon brick, towering around him, echoing Pink Floyd's anthem. "I couldn't," he said, voice cracking, whiskey searing his throat. Excuses—schedules, exhaustion—withered under the truth: shame, fear of facing what he'd chosen. At the crossroads. The path off no more than a degree. He punctuated it with an unsteady resolve, "Just feeling... gone."

Doc's hand tightened, sage-like. "Abuela'd say you're never gone," he said, eyes piercing. "God's calling, but you gotta answer."

Dante pushed him away, grabbing a bottle. "This is our life now," he said, voice flat. In a Nashville diner, the tour paused. Dante sat at the counter, coffee cold, an old jukebox thumping out Springsteen's *Born to Run*, its reckless abandon once his soul's spark, now a taunt of what he'd lost. Doubt sneered, his soul a ledger of loss—Bea's silence, the band's strain, the music hall's grace abandoned. The waitress, apron stained, eyed him with pity. "You look like you're carrying the world, hon," she said, sliding a refill he didn't touch.

In a dim-lit corner, Nico sat with his sketchbook open, pencil smudges shadowing his fingertips. Dante slid into the booth across from him, the diner's clatter muffled by the weight Nico carried. For a long moment he only stared at the page, jaw tight, then the memory broke loose in fragments.

"We were kids," he said, voice low, almost lost beneath the hiss of the griddle. His hand tapped the sketchbook, restless. "Elena and me—pots and pans in the garage. That was our band." A ghost of a smile flickered, then collapsed. "Last time I saw her, she was clean. Eyes bright. Swore she'd stay that way. She hugged me and said... *'This is final.'*"

The word hovered. He whispered it again, softer, like he was testing its weight in the air. "Final." His thumb dragged along the paper's edge. "She kept saying it—like she needed me to hold it with her. Like if we both believed it, it would be real."

Dante stilled. Nico, who had always drifted on the edges—silent, untouchable, speaking in fragments like smoke—was pouring out full sentences now, and each one landed like a hammer. This wasn't small talk. It was as if some wall inside him had cracked, and through the break poured something heavier than words. He felt the force of it—the quiet command Nico carried, a presence that rose above the shadows instead of being consumed by them. These weren't just memories being spilled; they were gifts, costly because of what they'd cost him. And for the first time, Dante got Nico, the sound in his soul, running deeper than crowds or stages, deeper even than grief. It felt prophetic. Nico wasn't only telling his story but delivering something meant for Dante—a word that carried weight beyond the room. He was listening.

"Couple nights later," Nico went on, voice fraying, "she called. Asked if I'd come hang out. She never asked that." His jaw clenched. "There was something in her voice. I heard it. I asked if she was okay. She paused—too long. Then said yeah." His fingers smudged the sketchbook, grinding the page. "I let it go. Pretended the pause didn't matter."

Dante's knuckles whitened against the table. He knew that evasion—the way shadows whispered.

"My car was in the shop," he said, throat working. "She was a couple miles away. I could've walked." His voice cracked. "I could have walked. I should have walked." His hand pressed to his forehead, shoulders shaking now. The word broke from him again, jagged but insistent: *"Final."*

He steadied, eyes blurring over the sketch. "Overdose." The word hit the air like a verdict. "That word... *final*... it never left me. In a world drowning in noise, it became something else. Her voice still saying: don't waste it. Don't sell your soul for what fades."

At last he looked up, gaze locking on Dante's. "That's why I play. For her. For what's real—not the crowds, not the hype. The part of the song that survives when the lights go dark. The thing that's still there when everything else burns away. When it matters most, when something cuts through all the smoke..." His voice steadied, luminous. "I say it."

The word fell between them, iron and fire both: *Final.*

Dante just stared, words snagging in his throat. He felt it strike deeper than applause ever had—not just Nico's story, but his own, laid bare in a single syllable. His chest rose, shuddering. Finally he broke: "I'm drowning. Bea's gone, and I can't stop."

Nico slid the sketchbook across the table. On the page: a piano in a ruined hall, light breaking through. "Find it," he said, eyes fierce, like dawn refusing the dark.

It lingered in Dante's bones like a toll, undeniable. Not condemnation, but inheritance. The word had reached into his being and named the ache he'd buried—the music hall's piano, Bea's light, the boy he'd been. He thought of Maria's arms, Paul's steady hand, the way home had always meant belonging even when he'd run. For a moment, the roar of the stage fell silent, the shadow's grip loosened, Something pulling him from the inferno's edge.

In the apartment's hush, his phone lit. *Dr. Caldwell: Beatrice is performing tomorrow. She's struggling. She needs you.* The words spoke. With new eyes he could see. How the depth of his valleys paved heights. How Bea's distance wasn't separation; it was a summons. How through it all, in it all, was not absence, but One who is.

A whisper broke from him, fragile yet certain: "Oh, God." A warm tide pulled him under and broke him open. He bowed his head, the word torn from him. A pause, heavier than silence. More passionate and resonant than anything he had ever sung. "My God!"

Nico's *Final* echoed—not condemnation, but revelation.

It was time to climb.

Chapter 8: The Mountain and the Flame

Columbus lay hushed, a ghost town under the tour's fleeting pause. The apartment was silent, but the photos were not. What once seemed fixed in frames, frozen in time, now stirred with a presence he could not escape. Each image seemed to breathe, lit from within—not mere memories but messengers, voices threading into the quiet. Compared to the fog of that other world—the shrine of rock gods he had joined—this small corner spoke differently. No dazzle. No hunger. Only home.

Grandpa Michael's knowing eyes fixed him with a gaze that felt like earnest counsel. Beside him, Catherine's faded portrait glowed with a faith that seemed to echo in Lake Diane's dawns. Paul and Maria, Rob and Anna's laughter, mid-picnic, shimmered warm as coffee steam curling from the lakehouse deck. Ben's grin, Tessa's calm joy, Sophia's wise counsel, cousins with guitars and violins under Michigan stars—each face alive, humming a truth older than applause. And Bea—her smile luminous, violin case slung over her shoulder—rose like the sunrise, her last text—*Grandma's gone. I needed you*—a wound searing. Yet the shelf offered no condemnation, only invitation—life calling life, a chorus waiting to be heard. Where hunger had ruled, grace whispered, summoning him to rise.

That evening, Bea stood in Dr. Caldwell's study, the air heavy with his expectations. "Beatrice, your performance tomorrow must be flawless," he said, voice crisp. "The conservatory depends on it." Her father sat behind his desk, glasses perched low, shuffling through a stack of gala notes. She stood there for a moment, heart pounding, then found her voice.

Her eyes flashed, but her tone was steady.

"Dad, I love you. And as much as I've longed for your affection, I've settled for your approval. I'm not your star. I'm your daughter. I want you to see me—not as you want me to be, but as I am."

The words spilled out like a dam breaking, years of restraint suddenly poured into the room.

"I didn't even have words for this until Dante's song broke through. I've been that caged bird. And I can't stay there. I need to play for what's inside of me—for truth, not for your donors."

Her words hung there, unrelenting, unpolished, but burning with a fire that was finally her own. For a moment, Dr. Caldwell did not look up. His fingers lingered on his papers too long, his posture rigid as though to resist the weight of her plea. When he finally lifted his eyes, they were softer, unguarded for just a breath. In that flicker Bea saw it: grief he'd never spoken, the loss of her mother—his late wife—a shadow holding his gaze. Bea's fire reminded him too much of the woman he had lost, and never truly mourned. Something in him cracked. His lips parted as if words might come, but none did.

The silence grew unbearable. He shifted, shoulders stiffening, retreating behind the only wall he knew: control. "I...," he began, the sound strained, almost alien in his mouth. He rose quickly, too quickly, brushing past her, his voice tight, his steps already pulling him toward the door. "Play your truth, then."

And then he was gone, the air trailing with his conflicted retreat—part yield, part flight.

Bea stood rooted, her heart racing. Had she broken something open—or broken something altogether? Fear pressed in, whispering she had gone too far. But in the stillness that followed, another voice whispered deeper, gentler. She closed her eyes, her hand tightening on the violin case like a prayer. She had spoken truth. She had to trust that was enough.

The band gathered at the apartment, air thick with tension. Jax leaned against the wall, smirk brittle, eyes hungry. He'd grown up with nothing, strumming a borrowed guitar in a cold apartment, dreaming of stages to escape hunger's bite. Fred tuned his bass, warmth dimmed, stare heavy. Nico sat, sketchbook open to a blank page. Doc stood by the window, his silence a weight. "We're losing it," Dante said, voice raw, breaking the quiet. "This tour, Lucian—it's killing us."

Jax scoffed, ambition a storm. "Speak for yourself. This is the dream—arenas, money, fame, the ladies. You wanna throw it away?"

Dante met his gaze, Bea's glow mysteriously emerging, the shadow dissipating. "It's not a dream," he said, voice steady. "It's a prison. Look at us—drunk, high, fighting. The Stones said it— *Shattered,* all those legends who fell. We've become marionettes, Jax, dangling for Lucian, for crowds who don't know us. We're brothers, not puppets."

Fred nodded, his eyes clearing. "He's right," he said, voice low. "I'm tired, man. Tired of losing you." Nico looked up, his empty page a promise. "It's hollow," he said, voice soft. "I'm in."

Jax's jaw tightened, but he saw their faces, the resolve in Dante's eyes, and faltered. "You're crazy," he said, but his voice softened, a crack in his armor. "Fine. What's the plan?"

Dante's heart pounded, the shadow loosening its grip even more, a spark breaking through the dark. He rose, voice steady at first, then swelling as though something larger spoke through him.

46

"We write truth," he said. "No more lies. No more Lucian. For us, brothers—for the heartbeat that brought us together. That energy when we first plugged in and something greater than us filled the room. We didn't invent it. We only poured it out. And it was worth pouring out. It was Someone bigger than each of us, reverberating through us, through everyone who heard."

He pressed forward, eyes burning, shoulders tense as if carrying the weight of every stage they'd ever played. His voice cut through the haze, raw, insistent.

"We've learned this. When the lights crash down, when the girls are gone, when the buzz burns off… in those long, aching nights when the noise dies and you're left staring at the ceiling—then it hits. We've had it all. Everything they dream about, everything they kill themselves chasing. And it's not enough."

"Truth. Right here." He struck his chest with the flat of his hand, the sound sharp, jarring. "It's worth more than stages, more than fans. You can't manufacture it. You can't script it, package it, sell it. You can only uncover it. Respond to it. That's what brought us together. That's the fire in our veins. That's our heartbeat."

Then Dante leaned in, voice lowering but weightier still. "It's time we live what we are. Live *Whose* we are. And with everything in us—pour it out. Lift it up."

The room stilled, their brotherhood flickering, fragile but alive. A vow took shape in the silence—not triumphant, not yet—but the promise of men who had touched the edge of lasting regret and chosen to climb.

That night, sleep drew Dante into a dream, vivid and searing, not of ash but of a mountain, steep and jagged, its thorns parting to reveal a radiant summit. Bea stood at the peak, her violin a beacon, its notes weaving a melody that trembled with contrition and hope. A chorus rose, not his voice but a multitude echoing through the crags:

Knees to stone, eyes to sky,
The broken rise where angels cry.
Each breath a hymn, each tear a flame,
Each wound a whisper of the Name.

The mountain pulsed, its slopes alive with figures—penitents
climbing, their faces scarred but resolute, their voices joining:

Can you hear the voices call,
Rising slow from sinners' fall?
They weep, they burn, they rise again—
A symphony of holy men.

Bea's violin soared, her eyes fierce with love, calling, *You're not*
alone, and Dante climbed, his sins—pride, betrayal, shame—
falling like chains, each step a prayer, each note a spark:

Regret like thunder splits the sky,
But mercy meets the desperate cry.

The summit glowed, a presence warm and infinite, whispering,
You are mine, as the voices swelled:

The sound that shakes the gate of gold—
The voices of the contrite soul.

He glimpsed Bea at the summit, their hands yearning to entwine,
their music a sacred call, a spark flickering against the shadow,
beckoning toward a boundless light yet to be reached. He
hesitated—feet bleeding, shame clawing back—but her melody
did not falter. He woke, heart racing, the Scioto outside his
window soothing, the dream's chorus lingering like incense. His
phone buzzed—Dr. Caldwell: *Tomorrow's her performance.*
She's hurting. Please be there. The words were a spark, the
dream a guide, and Dante felt the chain loosen, the climb
continuing.

Chapter 9: The Empyrean Light

The restored auditorium stood like a beacon on Columbus's riverfront, its brick facade polished to a gleam, its marquee blazing *Columbus Conservatory Gala* in elegant script. Once the crumbling music hall where Dante and Bea had played their duet, it was now a cathedral of sound, its vaulted ceiling soaring, its seats filled with illustrious guests—professors, patrons, city luminaries, their chatter percolating in anticipation. The Scioto caught the fading light, a silver thread weaving through the twilight, its voice a quiet hymn that called Dante forward, despite the ever-nipping shadow.

He stood at the back, ripped jeans and worn jacket in stark contrast to the tailored suits, his presence a ripple in the room's polish. He'd been here before. Dr. Caldwell's text had been a spark—*Beatrice is struggling. She needs you*—and the dream from last night, a mountain with Bea's violin at its peak, had been a guide. Grandma Caldwell's death, his failure to be there, weighed like yet another brick, but something deeper, Nico saw it—her light, their music, a presence he couldn't name—had moved him here, to this moment. To her.

Bea stood on the stage, violin tucked under her chin, her dark hair loose, her black dress a stark contrast to the spotlight's glow. The crowd hushed, her bow poised for a Bach Partita, but her shoulders trembled, her eyes heavy. Grandma Caldwell's absence was a void, her laughter silenced, and Dante's—had carved a deeper wound. Her father's expectations pressed against her. Dr. Caldwell sat in the front row, his face tight with concern, his pride warring with fear. The first note faltered, thin and unsteady, a cry stifled by loss, and a whisper rippled through the guests, their elegance fracturing.

Dante's heart seized. He'd ghosted her, run from her, but now, in this restored hall where their duet had begun, he felt the shadow retreat even more, a burning rising in his soul. He moved, uninvited, his boots scuffing the aisle, heads turning, whispers rising—"Who's that? The rockstar?"—but he didn't stop, his eyes on Bea. He climbed the stage, head down, the crowd's disquiet a drone, and sat at the grand piano, its keys welcoming his fingers.

Bea's eyes met his, wide with shock, then softening, a spark of recognition breaking through her grief. Dante played, not Bach, but a melody born in the Scioto's whisper, a call that wove through the hall like a river finding its course.

The notes were soft at first, then soared, a tide that lifted her. Her bow steadied, her violin answering, its voice a flame that danced with his, their music a harmony that burned through the room's pretense. It was their duet reborn, a sacred symphony that spoke of longing, grief, and redemption, a sanctuary where love and truth united, their souls entwining as they had in the hall, but deeper now.

Inside Bea, the music was a revelation, a redemptive rapids washing over her grief, her father's control, Dante's absence. Each note was a prayer, lifting her to a place where Grandma Caldwell's laughter echoed, where love burned eternal, where faith was not a fabrication or constraint, but a bridge to something vast. For Dante, it was vanquishing the shadow, the lies—*You're broken, beyond saving.* His love for her—deep, unspoken, sacramental—poured through the keys, transcending the stage, the crowd, the world's clamor.

The guests sat spellbound, their polish melting, some weeping, others clasping hands, as if the music had reached inside and touched a forgotten truth. Dr. Caldwell's eyes softened, his concern giving way to awe, his daughter's sacred passion a light he couldn't contain.

Eleanor Voss, the benefactor from the fundraiser, leaned forward, her face radiant, seeing the truth she'd glimpsed before. The music swelled, piano and violin a single voice, majestic and untamed, carrying the hall to a place where time paused, where only love and truth remained. The final note hung, a star in the silence, and the auditorium exhaled, applause rising like a tide, not polite but fervent.

Dante turned to Bea, tears shining in his eyes, his heart conquered, risen, utterly given. His lips formed the words that had been left unanswered: *I love you.* Bea gasped softly, her hand lifting to her mouth, tears spilling with abandon. She mouthed the words back, *I love you,* her gaze steady, sealing what the music had already declared.

As the applause continued in unrelenting waves, Bea stepped to Dante, her smile radiant through tears, and squeezed his hand. "You came," she whispered, voice trembling, her eyes peering into his soul. "For us."

"For you," Dante said, his voice tender, his heart unguarded, his eyes alight with radiance without shadow. "And yes, for us."

Dr. Caldwell approached, his voice low, his eyes misty. "Beatrice, Mr. Johnson—you've shown us something... extraordinary." It was a surrender, a father's love yielding to his daughter's truth, and Dante nodded, grateful, the boy who'd loved Bea now a man, his path clear.

In the back, the band awaited, summoned earlier by Doc to stand with their brother. Nico, tears streaming down his face, intoned what they had all just witnessed. "That... was... amazing."

Doc grinned. Fred nodded. Jax's eyes softened. "We're with you," he said, voice low and solemn.

And Dante felt their brotherhood—a bond forged in fire.

Lucian's text came—*You're throwing it away.* For a moment, the lie flickered. The applause. The fame. But Bea's hand was in his. The truth was burning. He deleted it and walked on, the hall's echo stronger, Bea's entire being seeming to glow.

They walked the Scioto's banks that night, hands woven, their love a sacred hymn. The river shimmered under the stars, their footsteps a rhythm that carried them toward a shared destiny. Bea paused, her eyes tender. "This is the overture," she said, voice steady. "Our real song begins." Dante, overcome by the enormity of it all, simply nodded. In that moment, they clearly recognized in themselves the unveiling reality of Something greater. God.

That night, sleep drew Dante into a dream, vivid and radiant, a paradiso. He stood in a boundless empyrean, a sea of blazing light, stars pulsing like chords of divine song. Bea was beside him, her violin weaving a melody that soared, a spark of eternal flame, their music a chorus that joined the heavens. "Blazing fire divine," their voices sang, echoing the song they'd forged, "eternal light, our souls entwine." A presence enveloped them, warm, infinite, whispering, *You are mine, forever home.* The stars danced about them, a reflection of the Maker's glory, transcending time. He woke, dawn's glow painting the room, filled with the anticipation of Bea's breath to be a melody soon beside him, his heart a flame that burned clear, the empyrean's light a truth he'd carry.

Chapter 10: Eternal Embrace

The Scioto shimmered like molten silver under a dawn-brushed sky, its current weaving past St. Joseph's Cathedral as if time itself flowed toward eternity. The church stood solemn, its bell towers casting shadows across downtown Columbus, a quiet summons to heaven's edge. Inside, the nave breathed incense and anticipation, the scent of ancient stone mingling with fresh lilies—earth and divine entwined. Organ notes swelled, and the congregation rose.

Dante Johnson stood at the altar, posture steady yet humble, dark curls neat, eyes alight with a hard-won radiance. His black suit, tailored but faintly rumpled, spoke of a man here not for show but for fidelity. He had descended into fame's inferno, been broken by its shadows, and now stood resurrected, a temple rebuilt by grace.

The doors parted, and the air held its breath.

Beatrice Caldwell—her name a whisper of blessing—glided down the marble aisle, each step a note in a melody composed since Eden. Her white dress flowed like a river, her veil a soft hymn trailing behind. The gathered—Paul and Maria, their faces warm with memory; Doc, red beanie skewed, rosary tattoo glinting; Fred, steady as stone; Jax, leather jacket swapped for a suit, eyes softened; Nico, sketching in his mind, a faint smile breaking through; Ben and Tessa with their families—felt it. This was no mere ceremony. It was liturgy. Not just romance, but resurrection.

Bea's eyes locked with Dante's—fierce, unflinching, ablaze with knowing. These were the eyes that had seen him lost in the blaze of crowds, waited through his silence, prayed through his shadows, and still burned with the spark that once wove their teenage hymns. Their hands met, a current passing between them, and the cathedral exhaled.

Father Wilson stood before them, his presence warm yet commanding, his wit setting a relational tone for the sacred. He scanned the faces, as if glimpsing a truth beyond the moment, then leaned forward, voice rich as aged oak. "Blessedness comes through brokenness," he said, gesturing to the crucifix above the altar, its wood scarred yet radiant. "The greatest gift God gives is Himself—broken, poured out, the very pulse of blessing."

Dante felt Bea's hand tighten, her warmth anchoring him. Father Wilson's gaze settled on them, steady and kind. "Blessedness comes through brokenness," he repeated, his voice a low bell, resonant with love's insistence. "G.K. Chesterton once wrote that the sun rises each morning not out of monotony, but out of God's relentless delight—a lover's vow renewed daily, a song that never tires. So too, this truth: blessedness comes through brokenness. It is not cold repetition, but the language of love, each echo drawing us deeper into the heart of the One who breaks to make us whole."

A murmur stirred the pews, the words sinking like roots. Father Wilson's eyes held Dante and Bea, his voice softening yet unyielding. "Marriage is death and rising. An invitation to lay down self, again and again, so you may rise together into a love that does not fade, kindled by a Fire that never ends. Dante, you've known stages, crowds, the roar of adulation. But here, at this altar, you step into a vow greater than any spotlight—a hymn God Himself composes through you and Beatrice, a living icon of His outpoured love."

A child's cough echoed faintly, swallowed by the vaulted hush. Father Wilson turned to the congregation, his voice a quiet tide. "This covenant will be tested. Shadows will whisper, the world will beckon. But it is a fortress, sustained by the One who calls you His own." His gaze returned to the couple, intimate yet vast. "Blessedness comes through brokenness. This is not performance, but presence—a song begun here, to be perfected when Love Himself welcomes you home."

Their vows were a sacred exchange, rings forged in the Spirit's spark. The Eucharist followed—bread and wine transformed into Flesh, mystery into meal. As they knelt, a hush fell, as if angels leaned closer.

The veil lifted, and with it, pretense, fear, and fracture dissolved. The wall between them crumbled, revealing two souls once lost, now found in each other and in Him. Their kiss was not theatrics but a sacrament, sealing a covenant carved through pain, joy, shadow, and grace.

Bells tolled, doors opened to sunlight, and the Scioto gleamed like a celestial echo. The reception unfolded in a riverside hall, not decadent but alive—food shared like grace, dance flowing like prayer, laughter rising like a psalm. Paul raised a glass, his voice thick with blessing. Maria wiped tears, her smile a hearth. Dr. Caldwell, pride softened by awe, met Bea's eyes and nodded, a father yielding to his daughter's truth.

Doc leaned against a pillar, drumming a quiet rhythm on his thigh, his grin recalling Abuela Rose's hymns that had carried him through a childhood of loss. "Jefe, you made it," he whispered, his rosary tattoo catching the light, a silent prayer for the brother he'd never stopped believing in. Fred stood nearby, his bass-calloused hands still, his loyalty a rock forged when he sold his car for the band, now tempered by seeing Dante whole. Jax, his usual smirk gone, adjusted his tie, a flicker of his old hunger—born in a childhood of empty cupboards—giving way to a quieter resolve, shaped by the band's shared climb. Nico, eyes bright with unshed tears, clutched his sketchbook, its pages holding a piano in a ruined hall, a spark he'd carried for Elena, now kindled anew in this moment of brotherhood.

55

Late into the night, as stars draped the sky and fireflies danced like grace notes, Dante took the microphone, Bea at his side, her violin cradled. "We've all walked through fire," he said, voice steady, raw with truth. "Felt unworthy of light. But tonight, you've blessed us, believed in us. Now, let us give back."

They turned to the piano, no stage lights, no roar of crowds—just a holy hush. Dante's fingers drew forth a melody, soft as memory, fierce as yearning. Bea's bow met the strings, a breath igniting a spark, and they played *Whisper of Heaven*:

Whisper of heaven,
Breathing life to my fading breath,
Whisper of heaven,
Sacred song lifting me from death,
My Beatrice, my beloved,
Today we're forever one.

The notes rose, wept, broke, and healed in one seamless motion—not a concert, but communion. Doc closed his eyes, hand on heart, Abuela's prayers alive in the sound. Fred's gaze softened, his loyalty rewarded. Jax nodded, a sailor home from the storm. Nico's tears fell, his sketchbook a testament to a sister redeemed through song. Paul reached for Maria, their love a mirror. Dr. Caldwell bowed his head, his daughter's fire a light he now embraced.

The final chord hung like incense—sweet, aching, eternal. Silence fell, and the veil between earth and heaven seemed to thin, a shared glimpse of the divine.

Weeks later, Primal Fire would record their first album—a rock epic not of fame, but of faith, born in shadow, baptized in grace. Every note a testimony, every lyric a vow.

But this night, this wedding, was its overture.

"We were made," Dante whispered, voice a vow, "for this kind of fire."

Bea's eyes met his, radiant, completing the promise. "To light the world."

By the Scioto, they stood, hands entwined, rings sparkling under the moon's soft glow. Dante's heart lay bare, tears tracing the weight of their journey—sacrifice, redemption, life from death. One word rose, the word that had haunted, hallowed, and illumined their path, not an end but a seal, on earth as in heaven:

"Final."

Chapter 11: Always In It

A year later, the Columbus morning bloomed softly over Dante and Bea's home, a warm haven of weathered brick and wide windows, where the Scioto wove a quiet whisper of belonging. In the nursery, brushed in dawn's blush and gold, they sat together on a woven rug, the empty crib a gentle shrine to Michael, their son, conceived in the holy ardor of their wedding night, lost at six months' gestation. Bea's hand held a faded ultrasound, an icon binding them to a higher place. Her dark hair caught the light as she whispered, voice soft with wonder, "Michael's with us, Dante, isn't he?"

Dante drew her close, his calloused hands—still scarred from fixing broken keys—enfolding hers, his eyes alight with love and reverence. "Always," he murmured, voice resonant with awe, "with Grandpa Michael, Grandma Catherine, your mother, Grandma Caldwell, singing in light." Their acknowledgment was not grief but communion, a mystery and wonder that refined their bond, ever-present, God always in it.

Their story was rooted in the deep, imperfect fabric of family, a wellspring of eternal life, its threads shimmering with grace. At the lake house near Hillsdale, where guitars and violins rang under Michigan stars, these roots, broken yet luminous, had held them. Primal Fire's brotherhood wove a family too, threading Dante's redemption. The band had transcended Lucian's seduction, its music a spark that set stages ablaze worldwide. They'd forged their own label, claimed their tours, and birthed a movement. Arenas became sanctuaries where strangers found friendship, their voices rising, touched by a light that healed, united, drew them toward eternity—a living relationship, not ritual. God's hand always in it. The restored piano and hall, once a ruin, mirrored their lives, polished keys and ceilings singing scars made whole.

I look back on the miles, the years like weathered glass—
The prayers I never finished, the dreams I let slip past...

Dante's gaze met Bea's, her eyes fierce yet tender, and she smiled, guiding his hand to her belly, unveiling the wonder: five months pregnant, their second child stirring within. His hands, once coaxing rapture from strings, found their truest calling cradling this new life, his soul fulfilled as husband, as father, loving with a heart made whole. Tears of joy traced their faces. They sang softly, voices entwining:

He was always in it—
Every tear, every breath.
Every heartbreak I survived
When I thought there was nothing left.
When the night was loud with silence,
When the joy was paper-thin—
I see it now, with eyes washed clear:
He was always in it.

The song was their truth, a wonder woven with eternity, an unveiling of a God who is love, holding each soul in His boundless heart. The house embraced them, its light steady, the nursery a cradle for hope reborn. Storms would come, darkness would press, but through each other, they'd touched the Empyrean Light, God's inner sanctuary, a beacon to set the world aflame, their saga poised to blaze anew.

Author's Note: Beyond the Fire

The story you've just read—*Primal Fire*—isn't just about music, fame, or a prodigal clawing his way home. It is, at its heart, a Divine Comedy retold in modern form: guitars and pills in place of papal robes and *terza rima*. But the themes? They are as old as dust, as immediate as breath.

This story was born not only from imagination, but from my own lived experience. I can trace it back to high school, where I watched classmates slowly erase the lines they once swore never to cross. Friday nights carried the intoxication of belonging, but Monday mornings revealed the aftermath—shallow laughter, bravado covering emptiness. Weekend after weekend, I watched good friends blur the lines, belonging coming bottled, joy bought on credit. Somewhere in me questions burned.

And the music of the age narrated it perfectly. The Rolling Stones sneered out the anthem:

"Look at me? Does it matter? I've been shattered!"
The line was more than sarcasm—it was prophecy. The soundtrack of my generation announced the same descent we were living. From Elvis to Hendrix, from Morrison to Bonham, the list of shattered idols piled high, proof of what happens when shadow wins the stage.

Because the *shadow* is not mere imagery. It is character, real and active. It whispers in every backstage hallway, pressing us toward ruin. But so is the *light*—a presence no less real, always calling, often softly, beckoning us to remember who we are. *Primal Fire* is written this way on purpose: shadow and light as presences, powers, not ideas. They contend for us, and their outcome is written in our choices.

And rock itself has always carried both currents. Sometimes it mocked, tore down, destroyed. But sometimes it prayed. Sometimes it ached. Sometimes it named what pulpits had forgotten. Roger Daltrey's cry, *"Love... reign o'er me!"* was no rebellion—it was a psalm shouted in the only language he had left. Rock was in my blood for this reason: it told the truth of longing, even when it didn't know the Giver.

So when I wrote *Primal Fire*, I couldn't help but hear it in rock. Dante's songs—from *Dance of Desire* to *Always In It*—are more than narrative devices. They are the arc of the human soul, the very soundtrack of our own choices. Lyrics I had scribbled years ago became seeds. With time, and providence, they became an actual album: fifteen tracks, a concept album in the lineage of *The Wall* and *Tommy*. But unlike those, *Primal Fire* insists this: it is not Dante's story alone. It is ours.

Some will ask about the soundtrack itself, and how it came to be. The truth is that modern tools—including AI—helped bring these songs to life, alongside my own production sensibilities. I understand the hesitation. But think of Peter Jackson's *Lord of the Rings*—those epic battle scenes are not diminished by the modeling that made them possible. Virtually every song on the radio today is shaped by technology. As Neil Peart wrote in *Spirit of Radio*: *"It's really just a question of your honesty."* That's what I've sought here—honesty. The tools are only instruments. What matters is the song.

We live, as C. S. Lewis warned in *The Screwtape Letters*, in a playground of devils. Only now the tempter's voice doesn't growl. It pings. It scrolls. It whispers in curated feeds: "You do you." "Your truth is enough." It feels like freedom—until it isn't. Until freedom itself becomes the snare.

That's why Dante Johnson's descent is not fiction. It's autobiography in fragments. Every one of us has felt the tug of the stage—where applause tempts us to forget who we are. We've bartered silence, buried guilt under glitter, traded truth for relevance. We've stood at crossroads believing the lie that the

Ten Commandments were arbitrary rules meant to restrict. But as Cecil B. DeMille declared with clarity that still burns: we cannot break the Ten Commandments; we can only break ourselves against them.

For all the fascination with Inferno—and it deserves it, holding up a mirror to our own collapse—what captured me most in Dante Alighieri's *Commedia* was not hell, but *Paradiso*. The Empyrean. The light too luminous to describe. The intimacy too intimate to reduce. Not the vague afterlife of cartoons, but the blazing reality we've been reaching for in every thrill, every late-night craving, every broken prayer.

And this is where *Primal Fire* turns. The fire that once burned us can, in Christ, become the very flame that refines us. God could, of course, speak to us as He did Saul—blinding light, booming voice. Sometimes He does. But usually He comes another way: through cracked voices, through stained-glass lives fractured by sin, still radiant with grace. Through a Church wounded and yet chosen. Through flawed instruments like Doc, like Bea, like you, like me.

Because this is not myth in the sense of fantasy. It is myth in the deeper sense: unveiling reality. And reality is this—beneath every urge is an ache for intimacy. Every rebellion is really a cry for communion. Every counterfeit fire is a longing for the flame that does not consume but completes.

This book was never meant to be read and shelved. It is meant to be entered. Felt. Sung. Like a cathedral entered barefoot, or a concert where heaven brushes earth. It is an invitation to move from beckoning to beholding.

You are part of this Divine Comedy. You are not merely audience; you are written into the score. You are invited—not just to survive the Inferno, but to let yourself be refined in purgatorial fire, and then to awaken to the Empyrean. To find the God who waits in the wings—not to shame, but to summon you into a light that never fades. To hear, maybe for the first time, that the flame was never meant to consume you, but to reveal who you really are.

We are not lost songs.
We are unfinished symphonies.
And the stage is set for return.

~ Greg Schlueter

Track 1: Dance of Desire

Verse 1
Feel the beat—let it take control,
Lights go down, lose your soul.
Hands on fire, lips like wine,
In the sheets
Chills down your spine.
One more kiss, one more drink,
Don't overthink—
Don't even blink.
You never know
Who you'll meet tonight,
It feels so wrong it must be right.

Chorus
Take the floor—Dance of Desire.
Wanting more—Feel the fire.
Hearts ignite—Lose control.
Burn all night—Lose your soul.
No regrets—No goodbye.
Touch the stars—Kiss the sky.
Crave it now—Never tire.
Live and die—Dance of Desire.

LISTEN NOW

Verse 2
Silk on skin, no strings to tie,
Just fireworks bursting in a velvet sky.
Names fade fast, but the thrill remains—
Fingers trace electric veins.
The thump of the show still shakes your chest,
But it's after the music you feel the rest.
Shadows curl at the edge of the bed,
But you crave one more touch instead.

Chorus

Take the floor—Dance of Desire.
Wanting more—Feel the fire.
Hearts ignite—Lose control.
Burn all night—Lose your soul.
No regrets—No goodbye.
Touch the stars—Kiss the sky.
Crave it now—Never tire.
Live and die—Dance of Desire.

Bridge

Round and round, you chase the spark,
The music fades but leaves its mark.
She's gone by dawn, but you want more—
Another name, another door.

Final Chorus

Take the floor—Dance of Desire.
Wanting more—Feel the fire.
Hearts ignite—Lose control.
Burn all night—Lose your soul.
No regrets—No goodbye.
Touch the stars—Kiss the sky.
Crave it now—Never tire.
Live and die—Dance of Desire.

Outro

But is there more
There must be more
There's gotta be more
I want more
I need more

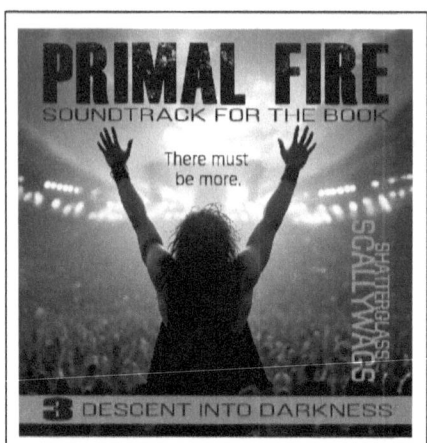

Track 3: Descent Into Darkness

Verse 1

I've seen the gates
Where shadows fall,
A silent scream beyond the wall,
They warned us once,
They warned us twice,
But now we pay the final price.
The whispers rise
From deep below,
A thousand souls in endless woe,
The path we tread is carved in flame,
The sins of man, they bear your name.

Pre-Chorus

The signs were there, the truth was spoken,
But lies were fed and bonds were broken,
We marched toward the black unknown,
But you were told—you've always known.

Chorus

Descent into the fire,
Feel the grip of Hell's desire,
The darkness waits, it's calling you,
And every word, it's been told, it's true.
Don't disregard the messenger's cry,
For what you fear is not a lie,
It's all been written in the stars and stone,
Now you face the void alone.

Verse 2

The ground gives way beneath your feet,
The air grows thin, the shadows creep,
Eyes of despair, they burn your soul,
The truth is here, it's taken hold.
The warnings lost in modern sound,
Now demons dance, they drag you down,

LISTEN NOW

Each step you take, the light grows dim,
The voices scream, "Repent your sin!"

Pre-Chorus
The signs were there, the truth was spoken,
But lies were fed and bonds were broken,
You mocked the words, you sealed your fate,
Now you stand before Hell's gate.

Chorus
Descent into the fire, feel the grip of Hell's desire,
The darkness waits, it's calling you,
And every word, it's been told, it's true.
Don't disregard the messenger's cry,
For what you fear is not a lie,
It's all been written in the stars and stone,
Now you face the void alone.

Bridge
The spiral deepens, the flames rise high,
Judgment is watching with blood-red eyes,
Your choices echo through the endless night,
You had your chance to see the light!
Witness the terror, it's all been real,
You laughed at fate, now you feel the steel.

Chorus
Descent into the fire, feel the grip of Hell's desire,
The darkness waits, it's calling you,
And every word, it's been told, it's true.
Don't disregard the messenger's cry,
For what you fear is not a lie,
It's all been written in the stars and stone,
Now you face the void alone.

Outro
You face the void alone…
It's all been told… it's all been shown.
Now you face the void… alone.

Track 4: Circles Of Despair

Verse 1

Step by step, the air grows thin,
Welcome to the wages of sin,
Where pride and lust, envy and
greed, feed the fires that never
recede. The weight of guilt upon
your chest, fools who thought
they'd never confess, but every lie,
every slight, pulls you deeper into
the night.

LISTEN NOW

Pre-Chorus

You thought it was just a tale,
Old myths to keep the weak and frail,
But now you see the pain is real,
A nightmare that you can't conceal.

Chorus

Round and round, the circles turn,
The souls that writhe, the flames that burn.
Don't pretend you haven't heard,
It's all been told in every word.
The truth was there, but you denied,
Now there's no place left to hide.
From circle to circle, the spiral's tight,
No escape from eternal night.

Verse 2

The glutton feeds on endless dread,
The violent drown in rivers red,
Wrathful souls in constant war,
They've forgotten what they're fighting for.
And the greedy cling to molten gold,
While slothful sink in endless cold,
Here's your future, painted clear,
The cost of pride is all too dear.

Pre-Chorus
You laughed it off, you mocked the wise,
Dismissed the warnings as disguise,
But witness now the endless fall,
Where hope is shattered once and all.

Chorus
Round and round, the circles turn,
The souls that writhe, the flames that burn.
Don't pretend you haven't heard,
It's all been told in every word.
The truth was there, but you denied,
Now there's no place left to hide.
From circle to circle, the spiral's tight,
No escape from eternal night.

Bridge
The weight of sin, it pulls you down,
The light's behind, you've lost the crown.
You had the chance to choose the way,
But here in Hell, there's no more day.
Each step below's a deeper fall,
The walls of torment close on all.
Now you see it's not a game,
Your soul's on fire, burned by shame!

Chorus

Outro
The spiral twists, it's pulling fast,
Each circle darker than the last.
The story's old, but it's no myth,
The truth is here—you're bound by it.
In circles deep, you find despair,
But don't say you weren't aware

Track 5: Lament Of The Betrayed

Verse 1
Beneath the frost, in silence bound, the traitor's heart makes no sound, icy breath on frozen lips, the deepest lies cut deep as whips. Here they lie, condemned to stone, where loyalty has been overthrown. Judas' kiss still lingers here, in the land where hope disappears.

LISTEN NOW

Pre-Chorus
You can feel it in the air,
Every whispered word of despair,
A thousand faces in the frost,
Each one knew the cost.

Chorus
Frozen deep in betrayal's hold,
Their stories lost, their hearts turned cold.
They swore the oath, they sold the trust,
Now entombed in ice and dust.
Every promise, every vow,
Echoes through the silence now.
The truth was known, the warnings clear,
Now they fall—there's no escape from here.

Verse 2
The wind it howls, but no one hears,
The weight of guilt across the years.
In shadows long, the traitors lie,
Bound by the chains they can't deny.
And as the ice cracks 'neath their feet,
There's no redemption, no retreat.
The blood they spilled, the trust they broke,
Now they drown in words they spoke.

70

Pre-Chorus
They thought the world would not recall,
But every treachery bears a call,
The truth that burned is carved in flame,
Now they're bound by their own shame.

Chorus
Frozen deep in betrayal's hold,
Their stories lost, their hearts turned cold.
They swore the oath, they sold the trust,
Now entombed in ice and dust.
Every promise, every vow,
Echoes through the silence now.
The truth was known, the warnings clear,
Now they fall—there's no escape from here.

Bridge
You laughed at fate, you played your game,
You thought you'd never taste the flame.
But here you stand in ice alone,
The seeds you sowed have now been sown.
The world it watches, the witness stands,
No mercy left in frozen lands.
The lies you wove now bind you tight,
A cage of frost, no end in sight!

Chorus

Outro
The cold has claimed the hearts of stone,
Their cries are muted, all alone.
In the darkest depth, the truth is weighed,
This is the fate of the betrayed.
Don't say you were never told,
When your heart turns ice, your soul grows cold.
This is real, and it's all been said,
The path to betrayal—forever dead.

Track 6: Mountain Of Redemption

Verse 1

Stone by stone, the path is steep,
Scars we carry, wounds run deep.
But every step through ash and
flame burns away the curse and
shame. The past still clings, the
guilt still speaks, yet grace is
rising from the peaks. No glory
comes without the pain, no crown
without the crimson stain.

LISTEN NOW

Pre-Chorus

This climb is long, the air is thin,
But mercy meets the will within.
We stumble, fall, then rise again—
Our hearts made whole
through trial and flame.

Chorus

Climb the mountain, feel the fire,
Every rung a soul pulled higher.
Chains are breaking, night undone,
The road of thorns becomes the sun.
Voices cry from deep below,
"Repent, believe, and let it go!"
Though shadows chase with every breath,
We rise above the grip of death.

Verse 2

Old desires try to pull us back,
Familiar lies along the track.
But eyes are set on purer skies,
Where truth is clear and self must die.

The mountain groans with sacred weight,
Each soul refining through the gate.
Forgiveness carved in every stone,
No one ascends this path alone.

Pre-Chorus
The angels weep for those who climb,
The dirt beneath is marked with time.
But every tear becomes a seed,
And blooms the fruit of holy need.

Chorus

Bridge
No fame will save you at this height,
No mask can stand before the Light.
Strip it all, let mercy sear,
And find the strength to persevere.
What once was pride becomes a prayer,
A burning heart laid open bare.
The climb is blood, the climb is grace—
Till we behold the Father's face!

Chorus (Final)
Climb the mountain, feel the fire,
Every rung a soul pulled higher.
Chains are breaking, night undone,
The road of thorns becomes the sun.
Lift your eyes, the light is near,
The dawn of love is breaking clear.
Though penance cuts and burdens bend,
This is the climb that has no end.

Outro
Step by step, we rise, redeemed,
Through smoke and flame, beyond the dream.
The mountain echoes through the air:
"This is the way—if you would dare."
The journey's long... but glory's fair.

Track 7: Voices Of Penitance

Verse 1

Knees to stone, eyes to sky, the
broken rise where angels cry.
Each breath a hymn, each tear a
flame, each wound a whisper of
the Name. No triumph here, no
swords are drawn, just souls that
bleed and press on. Through bitter
ash, through cleansing rain,
they sing a song born out of pain.

LISTEN NOW

Pre-Chorus

They are not lost, they are not weak—
These are the voices of the meek.
With every cry and every moan,
They lay their burdens at the Throne.

Chorus

Can you hear the voices call,
Rising slow from sinners' fall?
They weep, they burn, they rise again—
A symphony of holy men.
Regret like thunder splits the sky,
But mercy meets the desperate cry.
The sound that shakes the gate of gold—
The voices of the contrite soul.

Verse 2

They don't deny what they became,
But now they stand inside the flame.
No mask, no boast, no veil, no lie,
Just naked hearts beneath the eye.
Each step they take, a sin unchained,
Each psalm they sing, a soul reclaimed.
Their voices tremble through the air,
But rise like incense into prayer.

74

Pre-Chorus
These aren't the proud, these aren't the proud—
These are the hearts that kneel unbowed.
The shame they faced, the truth they spoke,
Now fan the flames of hope they woke.

Chorus

Bridge
Oh, heaven bends to catch that sound,
Where sorrow runs and grace is found.
Not in the proud, the rich, the strong—
But in the weak who know they're wrong.
Their broken hearts, their shattered pride,
Now shine like stars the night can't hide.
The angels pause to hear that tone—
A whispered "Father... bring me home."

Chorus (Final)
Can you hear the voices call,
Rising slow from sinners' fall?
They weep, they burn, they rise again—
A symphony of holy men.
Regret like thunder splits the sky,
But mercy meets the desperate cry.
And through their wounds, the light breaks through—
The song of souls who always knew.

Outro
These are the ones who mourned their sin,
And found the gate that waits within.
The world may scoff, but heaven stands—
To welcome home repentant hands.
So let the proud fall into dust...
But raise a cry with all the just.
The voices rise... can you hear them too?
They're calling now... for me and you.

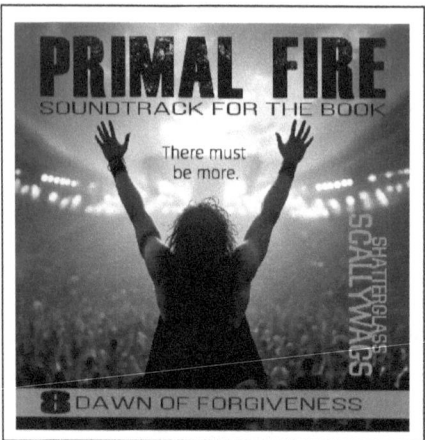

Track 8: Dawn Of Forgiveness

Verse 1
A stillness falls upon the hill,
the fire fades, the soul grows still.
The wounds remain, but not the
shame, a new day rises, not the
same. The weight that crushed, the
chains that bound, now lie in
pieces on the ground. A whisper
breaks the hardened stone—
"Your sins are gone.
You're not alone."

LISTEN NOW

Pre-Chorus
The night was long, the tears were real,
But mercy speaks what pain can't steal.
A golden light now warms the air,
Forgiveness found us waiting there.

Chorus
It's the dawn of forgiveness,
the breaking of day,
When sorrow gives way to the words You say.
"I know your scars. I've seen you fall—
But still, I came. I've paid it all."
The past erased, the shame released,
A rebel soul now crowned in peace.
This is the hour the darkness fled—
When love rose up and death lay dead.

Verse 2
You thought the light was lost to you,
But even ashes shine when true.
A single step, a whispered name,
Can split the sky and start the flame.
Now every scar becomes a song,
Of how the weak are made so strong.

No greater power could ever be—
Than a soul unbound, set free.

Pre-Chorus
You don't forget, but you let go—
The wounds become the seeds you sow.
The garden blooms where tears were sown,
The morning calls—you're not alone.

Chorus

Bridge
You can feel it in the air—
The weight is gone, the soul laid bare.
The light is warm, the sky is wide,
The King has called you to His side.
What once was curse is now a crown,
The prodigal is homeward bound.
So lift your head, the night is done—
Rise and walk… the race is won.

Chorus (Final)
It's the dawn of forgiveness, the breaking of day,
When sorrow gives way to the words You say.
"I know your scars. I've seen you fall—
But still, I came. I've paid it all."
The chains are dust, the grave undone,
The heart restored, the battle won.
This is the light we longed to see—
When love said, "Come and follow Me."

Outro
The night is past, the sun has climbed,
And mercy met us right on time.
You're not what you've done or left behind—
You are forgiven… now rise and shine.

Track 9: Celestial Ascent

Verse 1
No more chains to hold me down,
No more dust, no thorn, no crown.
The sky unfolds, the stars ignite,
I'm pulled into the breathless light.
Time dissolves, the veil is torn,
I rise in fire, reborn, reborn!
The weight of Earth now fades
below— where grace commands,
the soul must go.

LISTEN NOW

Pre-Chorus
The spheres are singing—do you hear?
The voice that drives out every fear.
From flesh to flame, from wound to wing,
I rise toward the Heart of all things.

Chorus
This is the Celestial Ascent—
Where glory flows, where light is sent.
No more shadows, no regret,
Just the music of the infinite.
Lifted past the realms of time,
The soul expands, the self aligned.
From dust to flame, from fall to flight—
I'm rising in eternal light.

Verse 2
Through silver skies and golden tones,
Past trembling stars and burning thrones,
Each sphere I cross begins to sing—
A chorus to the Risen King.
No sound like Earth, no air like this,
Just pure becoming—purest bliss.
The laws of man can't hold me now—
I bear the mark upon my brow.

Pre-Chorus
The eyes of saints, the wings of fire,
Beckon me to climb still higher.
No more fear, and no more night,
Only truth beyond the light.

Chorus
This is the Celestial Ascent—
Where glory flows, where light is sent.
No more shadows, no regret,
Just the music of the infinite.
Lifted past the realms of time,
The soul expands, the self aligned.
From dust to flame, from fall to flight—
I'm rising in eternal light.

Bridge
You were made to rise like this,
To break the chains of the abyss.
So cast aside the fading dream,
And climb the soul's ascending beam.
You were born for holy fire,
To ride the wind, to climb still higher!
Let Earth fall silent, let stars bend low—
The heavens open... and in you go.

Chorus
This is the Celestial Ascent—
The rising roar of innocence.
No wound remains, no curse survives,
The soul ignites and comes alive.
Beyond all time, beyond all death,
Beyond the bounds of mortal breath—
We rise, we soar, into the Light,
The Song of God... our final flight.

Outro
And now I rise beyond the skies,
Where love has burned and never dies.
Lifted by the sacred flame—
I rise... I rise... in Heaven's name.

Track 10: Vision Of Divine Love

Verse 1
I saw a flame that did not burn,
A light so pure it made Earth turn.
A voice without a sound or name,
Yet all I was became the same.
No shape, no form, no space, no
line, just endless Love that burned
through time.
And in that blaze I saw my face—
Reflected back in endless grace.

LISTEN NOW

Pre-Chorus
No fear remained, no need to speak,
The strength was found within the weak.
The Center called, the stars stood still,
And I surrendered all my will.

Chorus
This is the Vision—Divine and bright,
A Love that swallows death and night.
Not dream, not myth, not sky above—
But fire that is… the truth of Love.
You can't outrun, you can't contain—
This holy storm, this healing flame.
It's what we seek, it's who we are—
The burning heart beyond the stars.

Verse 2
The angel choirs dissolved in song,
No start, no end—it all belonged.
The mind gave way, the soul took flight,
Bathed in waves of endless light.
The truths we chased through time and tears
Were pulsing here beyond the years.
And all that hurt and all we've missed—
Undone within a single kiss.

Pre-Chorus

A kiss of flame, a gaze so wide,
Where mercy swells like ocean tide.
No greater bliss could Heaven yield—
Than just to look and be revealed.

Chorus

This is the Vision—Divine and bright,
A Love that swallows death and night.
Not dream, not myth, not sky above—
But fire that is… the truth of Love.
You can't outrun, you can't contain—
This holy storm, this healing flame.
It's what we seek, it's who we are—
The burning heart beyond the stars.

Bridge

You'll know it not by word or creed,
But when your soul begins to bleed.
When justice bows and pride is torn—
That's when Divine Love is born.
It's not a thought, it's not a fear,
It's what remains when all is clear.
A symphony beyond control—
The blazing mirror of the soul.

Chorus (Final)

This is the Vision—Divine and bright,
A Love that swallows death and night.
The voice that speaks before all time,
The fire that makes the stars align.
It breaks the sword, it heals the scar,
It burns within just where you are.
So fall into the heart above—
And be consumed… by endless Love.

Outro

Not far away, not high above—
You're standing in the arms of Love.
Don't look away…
It's real. It stays.
The Face you're made for… always.

Track 11:
Empyrean Light

Verse 1
I stood at the edge where time dissolves, where mystery lives and thought evolves. No sun, no moon, no flesh, no fire—just presence vast and rising higher. It wasn't light the eyes could see, but being—pure reality. And every song, and every star, was just a shadow of what You are.

LISTEN NOW

Pre-Chorus
Not silence, not a burning sky—
But glory thick you breathe, not try.
The veil is gone, the self undone,
And what remains is only One.

Chorus
This is the Empyrean Light,
Where fire and love and truth unite.
No more veils, no more disguise—
The soul at last beholds its prize.
Beyond all words, beyond all dreams,
The Light that is, the Light that sees.
You don't ascend, you are made new—
Drawn into Love itself… and through.

Verse 2
It wasn't earned, it wasn't bought—
But here the soul becomes the thought.
No shadow clings, no secret hides,
Just oceans made of mercy's tides.
Each saint, each flame, each angel's wing,
Just circles 'round the Endless King.
And stillness roars like thundering grace—
The echo of the Father's face.

Pre-Chorus
And in that gaze, all fear erased,
All hunger filled, all time replaced.
It's not ascent—it's being claimed—
It's Love that calls you by your name.

Chorus
This is the Empyrean Light,
Where fire and love and truth unite.
No more veils, no more disguise—
The soul at last beholds its prize.
Beyond all words, beyond all dreams,
The Light that is, the Light that sees.
You don't ascend, you are made new—
Drawn into Love itself… and through.

Bridge
Can you feel it pulling near?
The place beyond the grip of fear.
Where justice, joy, and peace converge,
And time is swallowed in the surge.
The Lamb is flame, the flame is song—
And we were meant here all along.
The door was always open wide—
But only love can step inside.

Chorus (Final)
This is the Empyrean Light,
Where darkness dies and all is right.
Where stars fall silent in the wake,
Of Love no soul can ever fake.
You don't arrive, you don't depart—
You've always burned inside His heart.
So let the veil be torn apart…
And enter in the Endless Light.

Outro
Not by force, not by sight—
But by surrender to the Light.
No more striving, no more night…
Only God. Only Light.
Only Love. Forever right.

Track 12: Whisper Of Heaven

Verse 1

The river's glow at fragile dawn,
we sang with childhood's grace,
Your violin, my guitar's spark,
one hymn in sacred space.
I chased the stage, fell to the void,
where shadows drowned my
flame, your fierce love, beloved,
broke the night, and called me
home by name.

Chorus

Whisper of heaven,
Breathing life to my fading breath,
Whisper of heaven,
Sacred song lifting me from death,
Whisper of heaven,
Radiant strings raising dawn's bright sun,
My Beatrice, my beloved,
Today we're forever one.

LISTEN NOW

Verse 2

Cold auditorium, cracked and worn,
where broken keys once sighed,
Your notes, my beautiful one, soared high,
our song no dark could hide.
Grandma's smile, grandpa's steady voice,
now echo in the skies,
Their love, like yours, a piercing force,
lifts splintered hearts to rise.

Chorus

Whisper of heaven,
Breathing life to my fading breath,
Whisper of heaven,
Sacred song lifting me from death,

Whisper of heaven,
Radiant strings raising dawn's bright sun,
My Beatrice, my beloved, today we're forever one.

Bridge
No fleeting spotlight could dim your call,
through hell's unyielding shade,
Your sacred fire, my holy one,
burned fierce where dreams would fade.
His whisper weaves our song as one,
to mend what sorrow tore,
Through us, His breath will lift the world,
His love forevermore.

Chorus
Whisper of heaven,
Breathing life to my fading breath,
Whisper of heaven,
Sacred song lifting me from death,
Whisper of heaven,
Radiant strings raising dawn's bright sun,
My Beatrice, my beloved,
Today we're forever one.
Today we're forever one.
With you, in God, today, forever one.

Outro
River's shine, our children's song
Will weave His holy art,
With heaven's choir—our loved ones near
His flame within each heart.
Whisper of heaven, my sacred one,
Through ages we'll ignite,
As one in Him, our song begins,
God's love, our endless flight.

Track 13: Eternal Embrace

Verse 1
I woke to a world draped in gold-plated lies, where serpent songs sweetened the skies. Desire wore silk and lips of flame, but every kiss forgot my name. The fruit was red, the promise bold, but rotted soft in hands gone cold. And all the lights that crowned the stage were shadows dancing in a cage.

LISTEN NOW

Pre-Chorus
But beneath the roar of every vice,
A whisper burned like hidden ice.
A Voice I'd buried, soft and grave—
Calling the child He still would save.

Chorus
This is the Eternal Embrace,
Where Heaven's King meets you face to face.
No matter how far into darkness you fell,
His grace reached farther—down into your hell.
He calls you by name and breaks every chain,
Reclaiming the soul you had drowned in pain.
Your heart's deepest longing was Him all along—
Now caught in His arms, you're where you belong.

Verse 2 – Beatrice
Then a light in the storm—eyes like a flame,
A beauty not born of fortune or fame.
Beatrice stood, not as flesh to possess,
But as truth in a world that had lost its Yes.
She named my shame without wielding a sword,
And showed me the face of my hungering Lord.

86

She turned lust to longing, my gaze to above—
And lit up the pathway that led into love.

Pre-Chorus
No longer chained to fading things,
My soul remembered it had wings.
Desire, once twisted, was now refined—
A fire remade in the Maker's design.

Chorus

Bridge
When I broke from the clutch of the night,
All hell quaked at the coming of Light.
Angels screamed and the heavens shook,
As the Lamb rewrote my tattered book.
The serpent hissed, but his crown was dust—
Unmasked as the thief who shattered trust.
But One stood taller, nailed and crowned—
And lifted me up from battleground.

Chorus
This is the Eternal Embrace,
Where death is drowned in the flood of grace.
No matter how far into darkness you fell,
His mercy reached farther—into your hell.
He calls you by name and breaks every chain,
Redeems your desires,
Makes whole what was stained.
The wound becomes wonder,
The fall becomes flight—
You're not what you did…
You're a child of the Light.

Outro
And Beatrice stood, aglow with the flame,
Not as the end—but the voice that called His name.
Through her, I saw the true Lover's face—
And fell into the arms of Eternal Embrace.
Eternal embrace. In His eternal embrace.
Seeing God face to face.
Seeing you face to face.

Track 14: Always In It

Verse 1
I look back on the miles, the years
like weathered glass—
The prayers I never finished, the
dreams I let slip past.
Faces flicker in my mind, like
stars I couldn't hold,
And I wonder—did it matter?
How will my story be told?

LISTEN NOW

Pre-Chorus
There were moments I was certain
I was lost beyond repair—
But through the silence, through the darkness,
A whisper hung in air:

Chorus
He was always in it—
Every tear, every breath.
Every heartbreak I survived
When I thought there was nothing left.
When the night was loud with silence,
When the joy was paper-thin—
I see it now, with eyes washed clear:
He was always in it.

Verse 2
There were hands I should've held,
And words I should've said—
Rooms I entered aching, hearts I left unread.
Still, something in the longing
Kept a candle burning bright,
A quiet fire I didn't see
That led me through the night.

Pre-Chorus
And all the questions I once shouted
Now feel smaller in the light—
Like stars you only notice
When you've left the noonday bright.

Chorus
He was always in it—
Every scar, every song.
Every stumble toward becoming
Where I feared I didn't belong.
When I doubted I was worth it,
When I ran or hid or sinned—
He was reaching, He was weeping—
He was always in it.

Bridge
Maybe heaven's not so distant—
Maybe glory's in the gray.
Maybe every holy mystery
Was threaded in each day.
And those who've gone before me
Aren't just shadows in the mist—
They are love that keeps on calling:
Child, it was always this…

Final Chorus
He was always in it—
In the laughter and the loss.
In the mercy poured out quietly
From a rugged wooden cross.
Now I lay it all before Him,
And I rise as I begin—
For the Maker of the stars and me—
He was always in it.

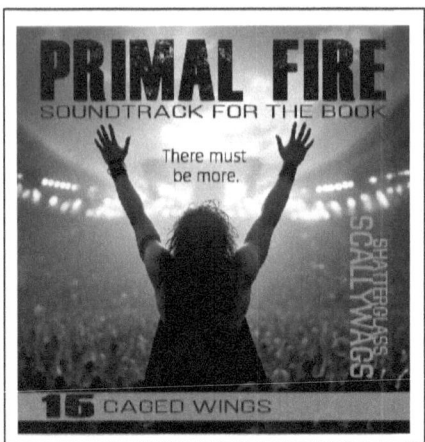

Track 15: Caged Wings

Verse 1
Here I am, wondering what you'd say, if I opened my heart—would you turn away?
Would you see the cracks where the light breaks through,
Where the prayers we whisper still carry truth, and call us to rise, to begin anew?

LISTEN NOW

Chorus
Caged wings, caged wings,
Meant for the sky, yet bound by strings.
Caged wings, caged wings,
Set me free—
From caged wings.

Verse 2
I see your faces polished, calm, composed,
But I hear the silence in the words you've closed.
Would you bare the scars that you try to hide,
Let the truth come rushing from the other side,
To feel, to breathe, to live, to fly?

Chorus
Caged wings, caged wings,
Meant for the sky, yet bound by strings.
Caged wings, caged wings,
Set us free—
From caged wings.
From caged wings.
From caged wings.
Set us free.

Acknowledgements

Music was in me from the start. As a kid at Sacred Heart School in Oshkosh, Wisconsin, I took piano lessons with **Sr. Rosaire** at the little convent next door. Though my brothers and I gave priority to chores, sports, and tormenting the neighbors, something in those keys found me. Before long, I was playing songs by heart—*Come Sail Away, Piano Man*—as if they'd been waiting there all along.

In time, another kind of music began to rise—made not of melody but of words. They came in torrents, often faster than I could contain. A blessing and a curse. Even typing ninety words a minute couldn't keep pace. Then I discovered the freedom of voice-to-text: the chance to speak the story aloud and let the heart lead before the head stepped in. "You write your first draft with your heart, and you rewrite with your head." That line from *Finding Forrester* became the compass of my craft. It reminded me of Michelangelo, who said he saw the angel in the marble and carved until he set it free.

My gratitude to **Angie Allen**, first reader and editor extraordinaire, who helped me do the same—addressing what surely was a boulder, and initiating the critical chipping.

To my beloved wife, **Stephanie**, whose candor, grace, and humor steady my wild momentum—she endured every patient reread, every late-night "one more paragraph," every bit of laughter along the way... *and still loves me.*

At its core, this story—and my life—is forged in music. One of the philosophers said that music is the language of the soul, and I believe that. Its rhythms and refrains have formed my friendships, shaped my faith, and scored my journey. There are too many to mention, but I must name a few—my **brothers in life and rock**: **Tom Branigan, John Davis, Dave McElroy**, and my sister, **Rachael**, and my own brothers, **Bart, Marty** and **Tobias**, but especially **Luke and Nathan**. I'll never forget that night on Lake Metonga: the moon on the water, contraband Swisher Sweets, and *Supertramp's Breakfast in America* spinning from start to finish. *The Logical Song. Lord, Is It Mine.* The soundtrack of our awakening hearts. And to later companions **Bill Noltner** and **Terry Langenderfer**, proof that *the long run* still has good company. True friends, like classic songs, never fade.

To all the others unnamed here but held close in my soul—those who helped kindle the fire in backyard bourbon and cigars, in solemn adoration before the Presence of God, and in every step along this long and winding yet sacred road—thank you. You've been part of the great jam session of grace.

On the odd graphic underlying every chapter—what may look like a simple line is really *our* story. Each of us begins as a single string—stretched and silent until touched by the hand of the Maker. Mysteriously, in God, every individual string is united: Dante's piano string and Bea's violin string reverberating with something more. Something transcendent. The sound hole and the flame mark the center of it all—the life of God, the source from whom every note is born. When our lives are tuned to His, our separate sounds become one music, rising and returning to the very Fire that gave them breath.

This is why we make music, why we long, why we love: to take part in the harmony of the One who first sang the world into being. In Him, every note finds home.

Thus, above all, to the **Holy Trinity**—the **Primal Fire**, the **Holy Spirit** who hovered over the waters and still holds all things in existence—be all glory. Every spark, every song, every story finds its light in Him. May this work, and every heart it touches, burn toward the everlasting flame of *Love who reigns o'er me.*

About the Author

Greg Schlueter is an author, speaker, and movement leader. In addition to directing communication and marketing for the Institute of American Constitutional Thought and Leadership, he leads Image Trinity, a dynamic marriage and family movement. He and his wife, Stephanie, co-host IGNITE Radio Live and produce the popular daily Gospel reflection at LiveITToday.us. He is a music composer, producer and lyricist at his recording company, Scallywag (find on all music platforms). His books include *The Magnificent Piglets of Pigletsville*, *Ride Of A Lifetime*, *Slaying Giants*, and the Johnson Family Saga of *Twelve Roses*, *25 Days*, and *Primal Fire* (find on Amazon). His personal blog is GregorianRant.us.

Squigglesprout

Squigglesprout is a media company founded in 2024. Our mission is to open souls to the horizon of the Good, Beautiful, True, and One through magnificent story telling. Find out more at Squigglesprout.com.

"[A] word on Squigglesprout, the most enchanting floral wonder in all the world. In proportion to the sunlight bathing its delicate form, the mystical blue Squigglesprout hums a melodic tune which, amid its august company on a radiant summer day, becomes a chorus reverberating through the air. Each of its leaflets seems to sway in rhythm, adding a whimsical ballet to the garden's ensemble. Its sprightly nature draws others near, inviting them to partake in its infectious mirth."

- *The Magnificent Piglets of Pigletsville*

discover scallywags

Anthematic Rock with a Soul

Deriving their name from the revolutionary piglets of *The Magnificent Piglets of Pigletsville*, Shatterglass Scallywags is my mythical band, bringing the human story with a masterful weave of wailing guitars, thrumming bass, drums thundering freedom's pulse and soaring vocals—a manifesto of love, loss, rebellion and redemption.

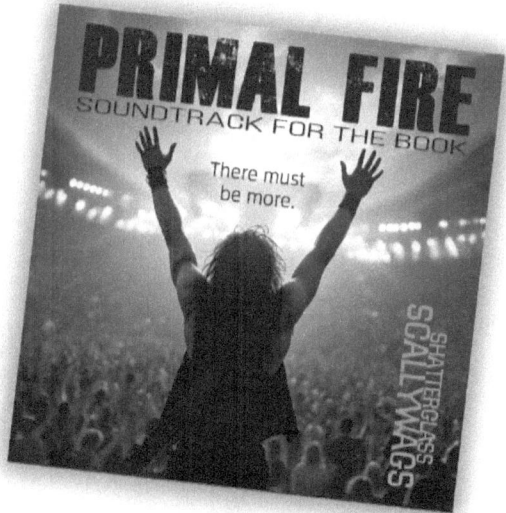

Composed with modern tools, including AI, it honors Neil Peart's wisdom from Rush's "The Spirit of Radio" (Moving Pictures): "It's really just a question of your honesty." As keyboards emulate real instruments and Peter Jackson's CGI brings epic battles to life, this technology enables my original lyrics and music to flourish, shaped by countless hours of soulful dedication.

Dive in, and let the Scallywags shatter your expectations.

enter the adventure.

Experience the Johnson Family Trilogy—three generations united by love, loss, and the fire that transforms.

A deeply moving journey through the seasons of life.

A prophetic glimpse into our culture's soul.

www.ingramcontent.com/pod-product-compliance
Lightning Source LLC
Chambersburg PA
CBHW030603130626
46552CB00006B/2651